A Tribalist Two

A Tribalist Two

Jefta Iluyomade

© 2017 Jefta Iluyomade
All rights reserved.

ISBN: 0692900136
ISBN 13: 9780692900130
Library of Congress Control Number: 2017908800
Jefta Iluyomade, Champaign,IL

To Grandma Abiola, for loving me in spite of everything I am not and could never be.

Contents

Tribe

*N*oun. A social division in a traditional society consisting of families or communities linked by social, economic, religious, or blood ties, with a common culture and dialect, typically having a recognized leader.

On my right the tribe attacks;
they lay snares for my feet,
they build their siege ramps against me.
They break up my road;
they succeed in destroying me.
"No one can help him," they say.
They advance as through a gaping breach;
amid the ruins they come rolling in.

—Job 30:12–14

Part I

The Precursor

1

YORUBA: Ọjọ Burúkú ||
ENGLISH: Wicked Day

Rays of sunlight glittered across the destruction of the Kialli village, highlighting the defeat of a once fortunate people. The hot
breath of a Domka soldier ran down the back of Khyik's neck. As if
that were not enough to remind him of his situation, the soldier shoved
Khyik in the center of an open wound carved into his lower back. He
did not need to ask where the soldiers were taking him in the heat of
day; he knew it was his death. He was the last son of the king, and with
his death, the Domka could rule without worry. Even if he were not
killed, Khyik doubted his presence would disrupt Mana's rule in any
significant way, but he understood why they would execute him. As
long as he breathed, the Kialli people would have hope. They would
have hope because he would give it to them, and because of this, there
would be great unrest.

The village was unrecognizable to Khyik. Even if his prior un-
consciousness had not muddled his senses, it would have looked like
a stranger. Pieces of rubble from the destroyed homes littered the

ground. The blisteringly hot sun overhead set the landscape ablaze. Sweat dripped from the faces of the men and women as they trudged in a line across the hot dirt road. Khyik was no exception, but sweat, he was used to. What he was not used to was the burning sensation in the small of his back as the sweat dripped into his wound. Every time a droplet slid across the open cut, he cringed in pain. Part of him expected an empathetic leopard to jump out from a thornbush and attack the soldiers, but the other part of him, the more mature part, knew that this was to be the end.

His baba had been deceived into trusting the Domka, and in the end, it had been his baba's final mistake. It was also Khyik's final mistake; he had been the one to suggest peace. Khyik was grateful that, at least, this village had already been pillaged, and any Kialli villagers he came across were either dead or had already been taken prisoner. Mana's desire, like that of all kings, was to rule uncontested, and now that Mana had control of the entire island, he could do so. Khyik looked up and squinted at the too-bright sky. They had come to a clearing, and the Domka soldiers formed a circle around him. Khyik looked left and right, trying to figure out why they had stopped.

A voice boomed from behind him, "Let me see the boy."

Khyik turned to face Mana himself. He was as large as men came; the pitch of his voice was as deep as the Elder River's rumble. Mana did not look at all tired, which made sense because his attack on the Kialli had been swift and nearly effortless.

"Ah, and here is the boy of the dead king," said Mana as the Domka soldiers laughed.

"I am the king now, and I advise you to execute me quickly!" Khyik yelled.

He did not know why he said that, but he was glad that he had. It could be true for all he knew. First his brother Orlo had been thought to be dead, then *not* Orlo when it was discovered he was alive. Then it was his brother Anen, who was surely to be killed by the Europeans now that the peace had been broken, then his brother Orlo again when he had actually been killed, and now it was likely Takloh and his baba, which left only him alive.

"Young man, why are you so eager to die? There is still life to be lived, and you do not have to suffer the same fate as your baba or the rest of his kin. I will allow you to live under my rule as my servant."

Mana's face was now close enough for Khyik to smell the wine that the Domka must have stolen from the king's quarters.

"You drink the wine gifted by the men who sought to destroy our people?" Khyik asked.

"You are the ones who accepted the wine," Mana pointed out.

"Out of diplomacy," Khyik retorted.

"Never mind. It is fitting. This wine belongs to men who sought to destroy your people, and it seems that today we are those men." Mana smiled as the Domka soldiers raised their weapons in agreement and cheered.

"We are the same people!" Khyik shouted.

Mana took a step back, drew back his hand, and slapped Khyik so hard that the sound echoed in the chaos. A drop of blood rolled down Khyik's cheek from where Mana's nail had dug into him with the slap.

"No," Mana whispered as he took a swig of wine. "We are not."

II

HAUSA: Ebo || ENGLISH: Tribe

Before...

Young children ran around outside of the royal kraal in their tiny clothes, for now he let them play in spite of their boisterousness. Obnoxious children always reminded him of his third-born son, Anen, who was probably up and about as well, just not in the same location. Anen was most likely pestering the chiefs about the meanings of old tribal texts until he either got his answers or used up all of the chiefs' patience. That was his third-born son's favorite activity, and though he admired persistence, he sometimes wished all of his children would act more like Nyari, his only daughter. Unlike her siblings, Nyari kept quiet and to herself. She acted well and did all the things that were expected of her, but the king knew that his daughter was inarguably the most intelligent of all his children. Just like her late mother, Nyari knew when not to be smart, and although he discouraged her from doing that, he felt a sense of nostalgia when she would play dumb to avoid getting in trouble, even if it meant her brothers took the punishment. As far as punishments went, no one took more of them than his youngest son, Khyik. Khyik, the scapegoat of the family. The king did not know where his son had found the knack of making himself a sponge for blame; of the traits that had been passed down from generation to generation, favorability was one that both he and the queen possessed. Not that his other children were not without their faults, mutual mischievousness for one, but his other children possessed traits that accented mischievousness. For Nyari it was mature intelligence, for Anen it was curiosity, and for Takloh it was pure, unmatched strength. He loved his son, but something about Khyik's vagueness, something about his son's disinterest in greatness, went against the very fiber that made up the rest of the family. The boy was clumsy and weak. He showed no concern for how he represented the family, nor did he show concern for how he came across to their subjects. Whatever it was that made his youngest son so unextraordinary, it was not a lack of exemplary role models. In the Kialli territories, there was an overabundance of laudable men—masculine, astute, tall like elephant grass, and island born. But for Khyik, none of these qualities came with age, so the king could only wait, watch, and be disappointed.

Khyik watched as his older brother tossed two men aside, though they were older and bigger; Takloh was stronger than both combined. Dawn had just passed, and the local pastime of roughhousing, which by now was seeing who was bold enough and stupid enough to challenge Takloh, was under way. Most of the men knew better; sitting in the shade, drinking spirits, they watched. Khyik kept watching. Every move Takloh made was well coordinated and backed by power. Khyik wondered how his brother had gotten that way, not that he had ever seen Takloh any other way. Even in his very first memories, Takloh had been bigger and stronger than most. But it was not admiration that Khyik felt; it was envy. He knew it was not good, but how could he not be envious? How could anybody not be envious? One of the men staggered backward to his knees and then leaped again at Takloh. Takloh dodged the attack, spinning around the man with ease before launching a counterattack. He was bloody and sweaty, but the men were not accustomed to seeing him any other way.

"Brother!"

Khyik turned around to find Anen walking up to him.

"Hello, brother," Khyik greeted. "Does the day treat you well?"

Anen nodded with a large smirk. "Only as well as the chiefs let the day treat me," he remarked.

"With you around, it's no wonder they grow weary."

The two boys let out loud laughs that were ultimately drowned out by the noise of Takloh's grunts.

"He sounds like warthogs in the mating season. Has he no brain?" Anen sighed.

"Would you like me to ask him for you?" Khyik opened his mouth to call for Takloh, but Anen gave him a playful shove.

"And you? Have you no brain?" Anen asked with a sudden change in tone. He turned toward his younger brother. "Crossing the Elder River like it was a farmer's fence that children climb over when they've kicked their playthings too far," Anen accused.

Khyik's mouth hung open, speechless.

"You don't think you can just sneak out after dark without at least one Kialli scout noticing? You're lucky Hiniri told me instead of Baba." Anen's face pulled closer so that his ears could pick up whatever excuse was about to be said.

"I was just a bit curious, that is all. And our animals cross the river, so why shouldn't I?" Khyik reasoned.

"Because the Domka won't slice open the bellies of our animals and wear their intestines like dress scarves," Anen reminded him. "So leave the curiosity to me."

There was silence between the two of them as they watched the last remaining man opt out of the tussle with Takloh.

"Your thoughts don't even try to hide in your head," said Khyik. "I assume you want something from me to ensure this news will not reach Baba?"

It was a reasonable thing to expect. Anen's specialty was gathering information, and he had learned that information was as good as any currency if used correctly.

"You know me all too well, young one. I do want something," Anen admitted. He lifted his knuckle to his mouth and gently bit down as he thought it over.

"Ah! You will give me entertainment," he finally said.

Khyik was confused.

"How so?"

Anen raised his hand and whistled, garnering the attention of everyone nearby. "Takloh!" he called. "The young brother would like to put you in your place!"

There was laughter throughout the group of men as shock settled onto Khyik's face.

"Is this true?" Takloh asked with amusement.

Khyik glared at Anen, who, knowing he had leverage, only glanced back. So with no other choice, Khyik stepped forward.

The good part was that it ended quickly. The bad part was the effort Takloh had to put forth to make it end quickly. As Khyik walked away, people either laughed or shook their heads, though one man tried to make him feel better.

"It could have been much, much worse," he said.

Khyik wanted to smile, but he was afraid some of his teeth might fall out. The damage was deliberate. Even if it had been a joke, a younger brother challenging his older brother would not be tolerated, especially in front of an audience. Takloh was to be named deputy in a month's time, and as his brother, Khyik could challenge him when the time came. That was out of the question. Even if Takloh had not been the oldest, if the king had had older sons of age, even then, Takloh would still be the undisputed choice for deputy. The man was right; it really could have been much, much worse. Khyik had seen Takloh break the jaw of one man and wring the ankle of another. He had seen his brother take out the legs of giants just as fast as he could bound straight over the heads of shorter adversaries.

"Why are you doing this?" Takloh had whispered when they were getting into position.

All Khyik did was glance at Anen, who looked on with eagerness.

"Ah, the plotter put you up to it. He has something over you then?" Takloh guessed.

"Yes, brother," Khyik admitted.

"Well, then I'll make it quick. Tussling with your own brother should not be a punishment," Takloh started.

The two put their heads together in a starting position.

"But it will be," Takloh said with a smile.

A busted lip and a semiswollen eye could hardly be called serious injuries, especially when tussling with Takloh. In all honesty, he had gone easy on him. Even when tempers were short in the heat, the prospect of rain brought out kindness. The dry season was nearing its end. The earth was as cracked as the parched mouth of a wandering nomad, but each day the cracks became less and less defined. The parched crevices grew smaller as each inconsistent drizzle not only satisfied the earth's need but also signified the sky's need for release.

It was on these grounds that Khyik walked toward the capitol village. The capitol village housed the kraal that housed the king. It sat in the middle of the village, and as Khyik got closer to the prized center, he could see his surroundings change. Small mud huts gave way to large log ones, large log huts gave way to larger stone ones, and where there were larger stone huts, there were polished wooden walkways to remind one of the lesser materials one had just surpassed by passing by. Then there was the royal kraal, made from every material available locally and from many materials fetched from lands far away. When Khyik reached the kraal, he found his baba sitting on one of his outdoor thrones, this one placed under a large bush willow that provided shade from the impeding sunlight.

"How are things, my son?" the king asked as Khyik walked up.

Khyik bowed a low bow. "Very good," he replied.

"Hmm, yes, so I suppose Takloh's beating has not put a damper on your day?" The king let out a hearty chuckle.

Khyik was surprised. "Baba, how have you known of that?" he asked. "I am only just returning."

The king shook his head. "You think you are the only one who attends morning tussles? Or did you not see men there? I take it they were not all hiding to stalk game? Many men tussle with Takloh for far longer than you did and still manage to make it back to the kraal faster. I think it is because you choose bad paths. Anyway, all of that aside, I have eyes. I can see your face. Only Takloh could be gracious enough to fight you so lightly. If it had been Anen, I would expect more scratches."

Khyik nodded. "I think you are right, Baba."

Children played in the compound, enclosed inside the walls that sheltered the building. They were not all privileged children; children of chiefs and farmers alike played side by side. Some days the kraal would be closed, but most days the king allowed it because it was the people's right. The kraal belonged to everyone in one way or another. As Takloh's deputy naming came closer, the king's chieftain council, which consisted of all the leaders of the surrounding Kialli villages, had suggested restricting the kraal as preparations were made. The king considered this and decided against it. He wanted everyone to be happy at the time of Takloh's deputy naming; the ceremony needed to be a time of unity. Khyik bowed once again to his baba and then proceeded to enter the kraal.

The kraal was a large building, the largest of any building in any of the Kialli villages. While too many materials had gone into its construction—a construction that had taken almost a quarter of a generation to complete—to name them all, the most prominent materials were smooth slabs of marble and acacia wood planks. It was a single-level building that was expansive almost beyond belief. The marble had been taken with much difficulty from mines located just a few miles away from where the Elder River met the South Atlantic Ocean. There were two such places where the Elder River made contact with the sea. There was a place in the north, which the chiefs called "the head of the Elder," where the ocean poured the wisest knowledge collected from foreign deities. The river then ran down the length of the island, splitting it equally in half, before finally meeting the ocean again in the south. Chiefs and other wise men of the tribe called this "the foot of the Elder," where all the knowledge of the island deities would be carried out to the rest of the world.

"Knowledge is garnered in the head, but leadership of the world requires a limb of action, the best of which is the foot"—this was a common ancestral phrase that men and women alike would repeat even if the topic of discussion was not the Elder River; the words worked to scold idleness as well. The kraal's interior walls were made from the thin acacia wood. It was most likely suggested during construction that some other wood be used, a softer, more readily available wood. It had no doubt been an inconvenience to the builders, but the aesthetic appeal the wood gave the kraal was worth it. There was no doubt that the color of the wood, an antediluvian russet, had paired nicely with the equally antique dress robes of the preceding generation. The wood made the kraal look as if through time the building had grown ripe and would grow riper still.

When he had been a boy and his mother, the queen, had been alive, the halls had been alive along with her. Courtly dressed servants still dashed around in an ant-like fashion, but not to do the bidding of a woman with a keen sense of style. Now when the servants ran their errands, it was always for something vitally boring. The king had been annoyed by his wife's choosiness of decoration and placement. He did not know it at the time, but it was this choosiness that kept the kraal from feeling like a kraal and kept it feeling like a home.

III

ARABIC: Kilyubatra ||
ENGLISH: Cleopatra

When Khyik found Nyari, she was painting one of her whit-tlings, a new one this time. Her room was the tidiest in the kraal, and she tried to keep in it only things that she used. In the far corner, she had her bed, upon which one silk sheet and one antelope skin were kept folded at all times, the silk for naps taken in the afternoon heat and the antelope skin to keep warm in the cooler nights of the dry season. She had lined her walls with her own watercolor paintings. Above where she slept was a plain landscape meticulously rendered in mashed okra, featuring a familiar glowing ball of gas, fire, and egg yolk sitting daintily against a white sky. In another area of her wall, a beige blend of paint was used to create a newborn springbok. In yet another, she had used real plumage to make a congregation of vibrant peafowl. She had some rugs that she had been meaning to get rid of... some clay pots that had been the queen's. Apart from those, there was nothing she could not go without—nothing except for her workspace.

The workspace only existed because of Nyari's wild imagination and her convincing the skilled woodworkers in the village to put aside their day labor so that they could help a little girl. Persuading the woodworkers had not been too difficult; she was a princess, after all. Nyari's workspace was a long table with many modifications that allowed for additional utility. It had taken several weeks for the woodworkers to get the design just right. She had wanted something unique, something that would aid in her self-expression. The workstation had to be broad enough to support multiple sculptures; at any given time, there were at least twelve items whittled from different woods, some brought from the innards of the bush and others from more accessible places, on display. There were also gourds on the side of the workstation; this was the most apparent and useful modification. They were attached by a thin but durable specially brewed honey paste that had no doubt been incredibly hard to obtain. The local bees were many things, but seldom were they lax, and they never took an opportunity to be hospitable, no matter how much smoke people coaxed them with. The gourds were meant for her many different watercolors. The largest gourds held the colors most often used, red and black. The black was based on thinned tar, and the red comprised a mixture of berries. The hanging gourds sat adjacent to other tools that she would use to sculpt the clay or fine-tune the physique of the wood. With her tools, she could eat away at grain relentlessly, carefully, until she saw curves in the body of block.

The village had many artisans, people who had restlessly studied the craftsmanship of the tribesman who came before them and had allowed their imaginations to dare to contribute something new, all to create masterpieces of culturally reflective art. The princess was among these people; she was also capable of making wonderful pieces. Khyik spoke to his sister only when there was no one to tell him to do otherwise, as so many people did, people like his baba.

Khyik did not know why his baba objected to him conversing with his own sister; perhaps it had to do with the disappointment his baba felt. Still it did not make sense; his defect was not of femininity but rather one of greatness. His sister was great. His sister was the only person to rival not only the dead queen's cunning but also her craftsmanship. She was a brilliant soul, and secretly he wished she would rub off on him.

Nyari was blowing the heat off one of her sculptures, a thornbush. He had not the slightest clue how she had managed to perfect the jagged edges or recreate the peculiar texture, but she had. She did not notice him entering her room, and when she did, she did no more than glance at him. When she was working on something, it occupied her wholly. Khyik sat down before her on the floor and ran his fingers in between the little sporadic hairs of a fine rug as he watched her. She set down her clay thornbush. She had just taken it away from the heat of the sun, which by now outside was nearing the zenithal intensity.

"I hope you didn't upset Baba."

"Why do you always think I've upset Baba?" Khyik replied.

"Well, have you?" Nyari asked.

"No, not this time."

Khyik smiled as his sister turned to face him. He did not have very many memories of his mother. The few memories that he did have of her were so foggy that he could not draw the lines between the definiteness of the past and the appetite of the subconscious mind. What was clear was that there was a resemblance between his sister and the maternal figment of his imagination that must have, at some point, been his mother. All the bold features were present: eyebrows like black rainbows on slightly lighter caramel skin, arching over big brown pupils that reflected images of the world; the contoured bridge of a nose that led to wide nostrils; and deep cheekbones on either side of a slender face. Yes, it was all there. She brought a sense of familiarity to an otherwise alien and distant woman he barely knew.

"I think what Baba wants is for you to get involved in something," she said as she looked at him.

"Is that all?" Khyik replied jokingly, his response accompanied with a scoff.

"Really, Khyik, it is not a bad idea." Nyari was the only person who called him by his first name, which was an uncommon thing to do.

The dead queen had often scolded her, "What rudeness lies within you! He is a man. Refer to him as 'brother'!"

Nyari never heeded the social norms and never gave them much thought, opting instead for an eye roll and getting beatings in return. It no longer mattered, as after the queen died, there was no one to reprimand her. It seemed scolding Nyari had been a task exclusively reserved for the queen, and so she was the sole woman in the village who did not call men by their titles. It was for the better; Khyik liked how Nyari spoke with him bluntly.

"I would suggest that you learn how to become a merchant," she said. "That way you can handle our people's financial welfare. Every day we trade more with the mainland."

She waited for a reaction, but a lack of one made her reevaluate her own recommendation.

"You have common sense enough to manage quantities, but with all this talk of strange men about the lands, I don't think Baba would let you step foot off the island."

Khyik did not have to ask her about the "strange talk"; they had all heard the bizarre speculations. Mercantilism, as it stood, was not on his agenda anyway, but he gave his sister a respectful nod and moved on to the more interesting subject.

"What do you make of this talk?"

He had not thought to ask his sister of her opinion before. Up until recently, the talk of strange men seemed to be nothing more than tales constructed from the overimaginitive heads of children. It was a common saying on the island that "too much free time makes a child's brain restless." Another was, "chores are anchors to reality." But there was a gain in the weight of words when they came from the mouths of men. Words from men could not be so easily dismissed, and it was now men the words were coming from.

"If you had asked me three days ago, I would have said what any other competent person would have said," she said.

"Which is?"

"Oh, I forgot you are not competent," she teased playfully. "I would have said, 'Leave the wild storytelling to the oracles because they craft them better! A man who lies for a living is more tolerable than a man who lies for an occasion.' Of course, three days ago Baba was not showing concern. Now I think that if they cannot be disproven, we must, for the good our people's safety, take them seriously."

He had not expected her to say what she had said. Nyari was smart. She was not as smart as she thought she was, but she was much smarter than everyone else thought, and the king was smart as well.

"Baba did not look worried," Khyik informed her.

"Good," she replied. "You need to understand that he's in a position of power. If he worries, then his subordinates worry, and then their subordinates, and so on. Fright—"

"Spreads faster than wildfire if the right people are the first to scream," Khyik finished the proverb for her.

Nyari tilted her head back. "Ah, I see you have been listening to the chiefs," she said, smiling.

"I listen to Baba, and Baba listens to the chiefs. If you are right and Baba is worried, but not showing it, then there has to be an ounce of truth in these tales," Khyik said.

"Khyik, when have you ever known me to be wrong?"

She turned back to her workstation to continue her work, and for a moment, the light from the window behind her recreated a lost silhouette. Just for a moment, the dead queen lived.

IV

NYANJA: Za Ena || ENGLISH: About the Others

It was less than a week later at around midday when the tribe heard of abominable occurrences on the mainland through a nomadic clan. The reports did not come from one single source. This time they stemmed from the mouths of many who did not call the island home. At first, it had only been one poor soul or maybe two small voices; trade was done between the island and the mainland, so news spread slowly, but it still spread. The king paid no attention to these inklings as his son's deputy naming drew nearer, and he had to focus on making sure it went smoothly. It was only when legitimate proof of these inklings—only when anguishing exhibit As and abominable exhibit Bs were advertised in the gossip—that his passive attitude and well-hidden fret transformed into deep concern. As quickly as they had been only rumors, they were now held as fact. The king decided to have a meeting with his chief advisers. Other high-ranking and respectable men were also ordered to be present at the meeting. So just two days after Khyik had talked with Nyari, all sorts of men gathered on the kraal's verandah to discuss what was to be done. Early in the morning, one by one, each man came. Upon arrival, they each produced their sitting stools. Before long, a sizable group of them took up most of the verandah.

"How does the day treat you all?" the king asked.

There were intelligible responses to be found in the cumulative murmur—apart from the cause of worry, most of them were doing just fine. A shallow bowl of drink made from coconut palm sap was passed around. When everyone had taken a sip, the discussion started. The men agreed that the rumors had become too troubling to ignore. One man pointed out that a village that had regularly traded fruits had not sent a merchant in three-quarters of a month. The king fretfully stroked his beard.

"So maybe the merchant has made off with the goods. It would not be the first time we would be subject to such treachery."

"Treachery is exactly what we are dealing with, but it is not from merchants," one man spoke out. "We suspected this, so we sent one of our own to the mainland village to request a new merchant."

The man speaking was the chief of one of the Kialli villages that was nearer to the mainland, a port village where merchants and traders would arrive by canoe to do business.

"How did that discussion go?" the king asked.

"It might've gone well if it had happened," the man replied. "When our man arrived, there was no one to talk to. There was nothing—no people, no buildings, none of the shrines the locals over there had placed."

He paused briefly as if he had not recognized the terror in what he was saying until then.

"Nothing," he finished.

An excited murmur arose. The king wanted to question further, but there was sorrowful certainty in the man's voice. His dark tone painted a sonic picture of the dumbfoundedness and shock he felt. Instead, the king opted to try to move the conversation forward.

"Needless to say this is troubling, but what does this have to do with these white 'men of other'?"

"Ah, yes, well, this merchant had been going on about it for quite some time. We actually thought him to be mad. 'White men with eyes like pale violets,' these 'men of other' who were traversing the land and causing destruction," the man explained.

"Even if he had been mad, you mean to tell me that no one thought it wise to at least humor him?" the king's voice boomed.

"I know we must appear to be the fools now," the man admitted. "But if you had seen how hysterical he had been as he went about his business, you would have been keen to throw him to the other side of the river."

"You shouldn't have been so easily disquieted!" the king bellowed. "Madmen are not so easily created from stable ones. Deterioration, especially of the mind, takes time."

The man from the port village hung his head as looks were passed between the others.

"It would be fitting to punish you," the king said after a pause. "But I will not. It was of good intention, and I suppose it is harder to heed a madman in practice than it is in theory."

The man nodded thankfully.

"These men of other—I take it they fight well then to cause this much ruckus?" said the king, throwing the question at the crowd of men around him.

"They use guns," an obscure voice said bluntly.

"Is that all? I should be the last person to have to remind you of how skilled Kialli men are in combat. It is a fact that we can wield our scythes as a third lethal fist."

There was a collective chuckle.

"Sir," the man from the port village spoke again, "we Kialli are unmatched. It's a fact that everyone on this side of the world knows. That being said, other tribes are not as fortunate to have our skills in battle. Most other tribes will crumble like young trees under the weight of elephants," the man said gloomily. "When our sister tribes in neighboring lands will have fallen, we will fight with scythes and blades as third and fourth hands, but we will be outnumbered and unallied."

At this, there was another round of murmurs. Women servants who had walked out onto the verandah to serve refreshments had heard what was said; although their closed mouths feigned disinterest, their faces gave away their intrigue. All faces in the room were fixed on the face of the king. His stare was intense, the thicker parts of his brows coming together as if upon their touch an answer would be created in his head. When he finally did speak, his words were long and drawn out as if he was merely projecting his thoughts as they came instead of verbalizing a solution.

"Hmm, their presence can do our people no good. Unless they prove otherwise, I think it is best to be on the offensive."

He did not shift his gaze from his invisible muse, but his speech had an obvious recipient—the man from the port village.

"You and all of the other leading men of port villages are to send messengers to the mainland, advising as many tribes as possible to treat these men of other as hostiles," the king ordered. "The only other tribe that could stand a chance alone is the Domka. This is probably why they have claimed to be at peace with us...easier to accept help with an open hand, I suppose, but allying with them is not an option. We need our sister tribes to deter the presence of these men."

The men around the verandah nodded in agreement. The king's orders held strength and purpose, and the king looked at his people as if carrying out his orders would make each of them hold strength and purpose.

His orders were carried out. As soon as the meeting was formally closed and bows had been exchanged, the leading men of the port villages did exactly as they were supposed to. They sent their quickest messengers on the fastest canoes available and sent them off with the message to treat the men of other as hostile. With the possibility of a war with outsiders, especially since previously the biggest wars had been with Domka, the king thought it would be wise to delay Takloh's deputy naming, much to Takloh's dismay.

"If you cannot understand how critical the situation is, then maybe you should not be deputy."

This had been the king's excuse and, to a lesser extent, threat. Takloh had huffed angrily and left his baba without any good-byes, but he had known the importance of the decision. He knew he was hot-headed, so he decided to calm his nerves by doing the only thing that could douse him. But since none of the men wanted to tussle with him when he was this angry—"The bastards," he thought—he decided to do the second-best thing: hunting. If the men on the island were scared of Takloh, then the animals were petrified. Maybe that was why he was one of the best hunters on the island; the animals he preyed on were too frightened to flee or maybe too wise, as if they knew that as far as human hunters went, Takloh might as well have been an omen of death.

It was a while after dawn, but the sky was still dark enough for it to be an advantage. Takloh decided to have one of his brothers accompany him. Khyik had not been his first choice, but he could not convince Anen to trade in his scrolls for hunting traps. Anen had poor hunting ability anyway, but Khyik had *no* hunting ability. He would have to do. Takloh just needed company so he could complain, and complain he did.

"I have been waiting for my entire life for the day that I might be able to call myself deputy and next leader of the tribe, and he takes that away from me—the nerve," Takloh whined.

Khyik stayed silent. Takloh butted heads with people often, but never did he butt heads with Baba.

"Then he asks me if I understand. Understand? I understand well and clear! If—" Takloh ended his complaint prematurely.

A bush squirrel, hugged up against a tree, had perked its ears up in anticipation of hearing the rest of Takloh's woes. Instead what it must have heard before its end was the sound of metal whizzing through the air and the sound of its own flesh splitting. Takloh's most recently mastered weapon was throwing knives—unusual weapons for serious hunting, but he had managed as always to make it work. Khyik knew that his brother was only human, but a part of him suspected that Takloh could hunt by word of mouth alone, as if he could order the animals to die and they would willingly obey. Takloh hung the squirrel on his waist, his fifth squirrel that morning.

"At this pace, you might rid the island of squirrels completely before the sun sets," Khyik remarked.

Takloh smiled briefly, his attention still on his next kill, whatever it would be. He quickly juggled the blade through his fingers, weaving it vigorously through his digits to display his mastery.

"Your turn," Takloh demanded.

He held out the knife for his brother, and Khyik reluctantly accepted. They walked for a time more, waiting for an opportunity to arise. Khyik looked up to see how far the sun had advanced across the sky, and this was when he saw his kill. A sleeping black-breasted bird nestled on a low-enough branch. As if Takloh had sensed the bird instead of seen it, he stopped dead in his tracks.

"It's within range," Takloh whispered.

"That is a blackbird. People do not like the taste of blackbirds," Khyik objected.

Takloh's face was solemn. "You think I like the taste of squirrels?" he asked, pointing to the collection on his waist.

"They taste good enough," Khyik reasoned.

"Not to me," Takloh informed him. "In the animal kingdom, there are some predators that will choose a live, unguaranteed meal over a carcass. We are not animals, but if we were, we would be those animals, and *those* animals don't really care much for taste."

Takloh smiled at his own statement, and seeing that there was no way to weasel out of the situation, Khyik took aim. He did not like killing animals, which further made him an oddity, but he did not mind doing it when prompted. In fairness, he had only done it one time, whereas his brother had done it one million times.

It had been long ago. He had been a little more than half of his current age. There was a village-wide feast, and goats had to be slaughtered for the occasion. He had been content with just watching, but his baba had insisted that he kill one of the goats. So a goat was brought for him, a knife was placed in his hand, and he did it. He made it quick. A farmer had made a line across the goat's neck with a dark sap, showing Khyik exactly where to slice.

That was different. He had never actively sought out to kill something and succeeded. Every once in a while, he told his baba that he had made a kill while out hunting with the men of the village. He accompanied the men several times, but lied about his kills. He lied often enough to make himself almost impressive—but not often enough to arouse suspicion.

The time that he had killed a goat, it had been quick. This time he was not so swift. When Khyik's grip loosened, it sent the knife hurling toward the bird in a spiral, not a straight line. The blunt-handle end of the knife hit the bird on its breast, instantaneously waking it. The knife pushed into the bird still spinning, and the sharp end must have made a gash somewhere beneath the feathers. The bird spread its wings and took flight, one, two, three branches tall, before the pain resonated. Then it came plummeting down in the same spiral shape the knife had traveled. It flopped drunkenly on the forest floor, its body thrashing violently against the leaves as its offended coos echoed through the trees, up the trunks, and under the canopy. It thrashed violently in a black haze, growing silent and then unsilent, alternating between the two.

"Well, do not just stand," sighed Takloh.

He pulled out another knife from his satchel and handed it to Khyik. Knife in hand, Khyik walked over to the flopping animal. Beady accusing eyes looked at him. Khyik squatted down and drove the blade into the animal. In an explosion of feathers, it disintegrated, one wing left of Khyik, another wing to the right of him. The beak, dismantled and hanging open, propped up on the side of a tree, other parts of the bird in other parts of the wood.

"I told you we should have left it alone," Khyik grumbled as he swatted away feathers stuck to his body.

Takloh looked as though he wanted to laugh, but his anger would not allow it.

"You are a lousy hunter," he said insultingly, grinning.

"You are a lousy listener. We could have caught something else in the time it took for the bird to die, but you ignored reason so you could have your way," Khyik argued.

Through an open-mouthed frown, air filled Takloh's lungs, but it stopped short of a yell; maybe it was because he did not want to frighten his brother with his full intensity, or maybe it was because doing so would have scared away all the game. Whatever the reason, he caught himself. He walked over to his brother and squatted down next to him, pointlessly picking at the scattered feathers. He sighed.

"I ignored reason so that I could have my way," he repeated.

This caught Khyik's attention. His beastly older brother, the adolescent champion among men, rarely showed his softer side. That side of him was hidden under expectations and time.

"That might just be how I acted with Baba," Takloh thought aloud.

"So I was right?" Khyik asked.

"Yes, brother, you were right."

Takloh smiled and rubbed the fuzzy overgrown hair on Khyik's head.

"I cannot recall the last time *I* was right and *you* were wrong," said Khyik.

"That is because prior to today, no such time existed," Takloh teased.

Khyik's head inflated a bit at the thought of being wiser than his eldest brother.

"And no such time should exist again." Takloh gave his brother a soft shove.

They gathered their knives and started back toward the village, Khyik feeling a little less worthless and Takloh feeling a little more humble.

V

AMHARIC: K'wat'ero
|| ENGLISH: Knot

Stormy was the sky.
A loud bang, thunder or gun?
Run, my people, run.

His window shade, made from mopane leaves and adorned with old amber tube beads, was pulled down all the way. As well made as it was, it could not keep the rain from entering his room. The water reminded Khyik of when he had seen weasels forcing their way into rabbits' burrows, naturally annoying the hell out of the rabbits, intruders one and the same. Khyik ignored the mess being made. His eyes were closed, and he slowly swung his hammock (he had insisted on a hammock in his room instead of a bed) back and forth to match the beat of the rain. He was slightly off; the hammock kept hitting its peaks on *tips* and not *taps*. There was just too much noise. Funnily enough on the previous night, sleep had eluded him because it had been too quiet; it was always too quiet when the crickets skipped choir. Just his luck that on this night the beat of precipitation was an antilullaby, the obnoxious notes of which were brash against his eardrums. He got up from his hammock, seeing no point in chasing sleep that only got further away. Inactivity had made his legs numb, so he paced the length of his room to get some feeling back. If the rain was an annoying beat, then the thunder was the wretched baseline. Its mighty hum had startled Khyik just as he was about to enter a well-deserved coma. He had not been able to ease his mind into rest since. There was a gourd of water next to his hammock, and he took a sip as he eyed the tiny migrating shadows. Sips turned into gulps. When he finished, he returned to his hammock and tried once again to fall asleep.

A horrific noise caused him to stand to his feet immediately. It was not thunder. It was not rain. It was human. It resembled the sound that men made when Takloh pinned them down too hard. It resembled the sound the blackbird had made when he had killed it, the final ominous croak. Rushed footsteps made themselves heard outside of the kraal. Khyik did not waste a second to find out what was going on. He ran out of his room and down the halls before popping out of the kraal to find that he was late. Many men, his baba included, were standing outside. There was someone on the ground who was enclosed by a crowd. The crowd was made up of mostly women. Khyik wanted to talk to his baba, to ask him what in the name of the Elder was going on, but various men kept talking to him indefinitely.

Khyik considered for a moment that he might be dreaming; it was odd that so many people were out and about at this time of night, especially in a storm. He could not see more than five leaps of a man ahead. There had to be somebody he could talk to who knew what was going on. He saw a hand beckoning to him. He could just barely make out the motion through the downpour. The hand belonged to Anen. Khyik walked to his brother. On his way, he passed the crowd of women and inspected the person on the floor. He heard crying that the storm had not allowed him to hear before. One look at the poor soul and his eyes were bombarded by haunting flakes of red on a static body. He could tell from the glum faces around him that absolutely nothing good could come of the night. When he reached Anen, they skipped their usual greeting.

"That person," Khyik said, looking back at the crowd, "they have passed on, have they not?"

"Hmm?" Anen looked back at the crowd as if he had forgotten what they were circling. "Oh, yes, quite dead," he said matter-of-factly.

Countless questions surfaced in Khyik's mind.

"Dead of what cause?" he asked, frustrated with Anen's indifference.

"Whichever one they felt the most strongly about, I would hope," Anen answered, staring off into the distance.

Khyik crossed his arms and huffed. Somewhere in the sky, there was a deity sympathetic to mortals, and the rain stopped. The last stragglers rolled down his face. He decided that strangling an answer out of his brother would only add another corpse. Anen never stopped talking, but whenever he did, it was pointless to try to make him, so Khyik joined in the silence. He looked at the moon, which was no doubt slowly inching its way out of view, it too a bystander that had seen the grim spectacle and made the choice to see no more.

"Those wild dogs," spat Anen suddenly.

Armed men left and entered the compound of the kraal in steady streams.

"It was the men of other," he said.

Khyik bit his lip nervously.

"They arrived during the storm and laid waste to half of a port village, the one in the north closest to the mouth of the Elder," Anen continued. "That man on the floor was their fastest messenger. He ran here injured to inform us of the attack."

Khyik was astounded. "It's a fourth of a day's walk from here to that village," he pointed out.

"Yes, but you would be surprised to see how fast a man can run when death is on his heels," said Anen.

"They used guns, I'm sure," said Khyik quietly.

"And we used metal. We captured them. I heard some of the men coming in say they are apprehended now and waiting for the king to decide their fates," responded Anen.

"Takloh?" Khyik asked.

"He was the first to leave. He left as soon as that man came tumbling in here out of breath, with half of his blood on the ground, screaming, 'Men of other! Men of other!' He took a scythe and the first able-bodied men he could find, and just like that he was off. Look, here comes Baba now."

The king and most of his chieftain council left the compound and headed straight for the northern port village. No one paid them any attention, so Khyik and Anen decided to follow behind. The company moved quickly. Khyik was at the back of the group, but he never fell too far behind. To an uninformed onlooker, they would have looked unusual, the king and his chieftain council accompanied by some guards and two young men jogging in the night. They all were relatively quiet except for the sounds of their feet shuffling against the dirt or an unmentioned piece of information that a chief had forgotten to tell the king; they drew no attention to themselves.

When they finally neared the victim village, a foggy smoke greeted them, flexing its gaseous body over most of the huts and other small buildings. Before they entered the village, the king, taking notice of his sons, instructed that two guards should look over Khyik and that he was not to be allowed inside; while his baba was not subtle, Khyik knew he had good intentions. Whatever scene lay within was not to be taken lightly. His baba did not want him to see the gruesome sights that might make a young soul rot. Since he was too tired to argue, he waited outside as the king, his chiefs and guards, and Anen disappeared past the smoldering aftermath.

Khyik could see the outlines of what must have been dead bodies in the moonlight. He could tell because they were similar to the one he had seen back in the kraal's compound and because the figureless heaps had the attribute that all dead things had; they drew eyes and demanded to be looked at it even though he himself knew that the image in question could only be grotesque and vile.

Khyik stood quietly next to his unmoving overseers. They had wanted to go inside the village, but they too had known that it would have been distasteful to argue with the king, especially in a time like this. Yet there was no lack of arguing. Khyik could hear it. It was between the king and Takloh. Everything was so quiet that it was impossible not to hear the gruff voices, the inevitable clash of their words. After a time, the voices stopped. The king, Anen, and Takloh, along with many other men, walked to Khyik and the two guards.

"I do not care what they deserved. When something like this happens, you subdue them if you can and wait for my jurisdiction," muttered the king.

Khyik had never seen his brother as angry as he was (and Takloh was angry very often). But that night, there was something to be found in Takloh's face. More than frustration, more than disgust, it was sadness. It was sadness cloaking itself with rage.

"Do you hear yourself, old man?" Takloh roared.

The guards next to Khyik, once unmoving, now shook.

"Look around you! Do I need to show you the dead again?" Takloh's voice cracked through the air like a bullwhip.

Khyik saw his brother's body, and it was covered in blood that was not his. No, Takloh could live in a fortress of thornbushes and still wake up every day unscathed. It was obvious that Takloh had taken matters into his own hands after he and his men had taken down the men of other. Even with everything that had happened, he could still be in awe of his brother—fighting unknown villains and being covered in blood, not a drop of it being his. The king closed his eyes tightly, as if reality was a bad dream that he could blink away. When he opened them again and found that nothing had changed, he sighed.

"Take me to them then," he said.

Takloh led the way. "You'd better come along too, brother. There is no use in sheltering you from justice."

He walked toward the whooshing sound of waves in the distance buried behind an assortment of fever trees. They reached a row of saplings assembled in view of the waves. The justice Takloh was referring to was ghastly and stood out against the beautiful curls of immeasurable water.

Twelve men of other hung from these trees, each one on his own tree. The men around him nodded their heads agreeably, but the sight saddened Khyik. What had driven these strange men to commit such atrocities against his people? The mouth of the Elder was also in view. Usually its sight pleased him, but not this time. There were enemies on the other side of that mouth in addition to the men of other, rotten teeth behind a delightful smile.

VI

SHONA: Uya Ne Enda ||
ENGLISH: Come and Go

Twelve trees,
Youngest branch no shorter than twelve feet tall.
Twelve deceased,
Bodies hanging, limbs dangling sprawled.
Twelve nooses,
Tied terrific, note their luscious loop.
Twelve graves,
Never dug, so twelve graves too few.
Twelve trees,
Oldest branch no taller than twelve feet tall.

Rebuilding the village was no easy task. The burials alone had taken several days to complete, and the construction could not commence before then. Even when the burials had been completed, there was little morale to fix what the men of other had ruined. Many people who had lost their loved ones during the attack decided to find new homes in other villages and stay with their extended families. The village's populace was scattering.

This was a bad thing economy-wise; port villages were obviously essential for trade, but there was not much the king could do. He could not force people to live where they did not want to live. He *could*, in theory, but he felt it cruel. It would have been cruel to force people to live among the dead. The bodies might have been cold, but the memories were still warmly animated. Were it not for the fact that half the village had become a cemetery overnight, the king might have hushed his conscience in the name of capitalism, but he felt their pain personally. He saw his face in the empty expression of a mother wrought childless or the scowl of a baba full of anguish at having lost the family that he had tacitly sworn to protect. The king could not do it. When the queen had died, the kraal had become an asylum of bitter nostalgia, so unkind was the taste that he could not swallow; it had taken weeks for him to step foot in the kraal and even longer for him to accept the eerie aura that clung to it.

"They need time away from that place. At the rate that people are leaving, there is no logic in rebuilding. Perhaps once the people's memories have faded a little, we might be able to reestablish the village." This was what he had said when asked about what was to be done.

He did not like to talk about what had occurred there. That afternoon, he had seen potent tragedy, the kind that left dark remnants in the head of anyone sane. He did not want his mind to latch on to the remnants. He subtly made this knowledge public by altering his disposition whenever someone brought it up—a change in expression or a hint of offense in his voice and he would not be asked again. So with its physical state unusable for business and with no one forcing its inhabitants to stay in their familial slaughterhouses, the village turned fully to ash.

The men of other still hung high for anyone eyeing the island's shores to see. If they had arrived by a vessel, then it must have fled because it could not be found. Their guns had been burned and tossed into the fever trees to be lost in the wilderness. Burying the guns had been considered, but the idea did not sit right with Takloh, who had thought it inappropriate that the weapons used for the slaughter should find rest in the same earth as the victims. Tossing the burned guns into the sea had also been proposed, but that idea was also marked as a bad one.

"The sea is the drink of the mouth of the Elder. Let us try not to poison the beverage."

With that, the guns were simply discarded. The village earned itself a title. People called it Village of the Twelve Trees, "where you can find either ghosts or ash." Anyone who visited the place would know one could find both.

With everything that had happened, nobody anticipated the arrival of more Europeans, let alone with such preposterous proposals at hand. Some women had been out collecting berries for fruit bread when they encountered more people of other; it was a small squadron. When the women saw them, they immediately ran. The king sent for guards to kill them. They would have been killed if they had not put their guns down immediately in submission, which they did. Unsure about killing the group, which consisted of only three men, the guards escorted them to the kraal. The village flew into hysteria. Women stayed in their huts, men as well. Some watched from windows, while others made it clear that they would not allow a second Village of the Twelve Trees and stood on their verandahs, scythes in hand. Two of the men of other openly showed their fear. The one who did not must have been the leader because he walked in front. It was this man whom the king looked to when they finally reached the kraal's compound. For a long time, no one spoke. The king, sitting on one of his outdoor thrones, observed the men before him. They looked unnatural, with their pale faces and features so opposite of his. The leader of the men of other stared at the king suspiciously.

"King, are you?" the leader of the men said suddenly.

This surprised the king, and for a moment, he was not sure if he had heard correctly.

"Where have you learned to speak our tongue?" the king asked.

The leader fell silent. The guards moved closer to the men to try to force an answer.

"We learned to speak it through friends who had visited this land," the leader answered, seeing them advance.

The language of the islanders was hard and clumsy on the tongues of the men of other, but the king was quite amused, impressed even.

"You have no friends here on this side of the earth," the king said coldly.

The leader of the men of other smiled knowingly. "I must disagree with you."

The king was not sure what to make of it. He quickly ran through a list of tribes that might betray the Kialli. At the top of the list were the Domka, but he refused to believe that the Domka, the same tribe that had poisoned his wife and kidnapped his son long ago, would stoop so low as to taint the purity of the island by allowing imposters.

"There is not a single tribe within our vicinity who would call your people friends," the king held.

By now a small crowd of brave individuals had gathered around and was listening intently. The leader sighed and then went on to list numerous tribes that the Kialli were allied with. The leader ran through names of other distant kings and chiefs; he talked about gifts he had received as well as goods that had been traded. With every word the man spoke, it became clearer and clearer that he was well acquainted with the people, customs, and culture of the tribes allied with the Kialli.

After a long while, the man stopped talking, having little else to say. He had proven his ties with the other tribes, and the king was furious.

"*I* have been betrayed then. The people on the mainland, I can no longer call them my friends." The king looked directly at the men of other. "I advised my allies to treat you and your kind as hostiles. Instead they valued my words so little that they did the exact opposite. Tell me, then, what reason did they give for you to attack the port village, or did your people just so happen to stumble upon it on your way here to 'make friends' and think it would be a fun diversion?"

The men of other looked confused. The king figured that he had overestimated their speaking abilities and repeated slowly. Still the looks of confusion on the men's faces did not vanish.

"We have no idea what you are talking about," the leader said.

"Lie to my face again, and die as violently as the people you killed!" the king threatened.

The men of other were shaken by the king's outburst, much to the pleasure of the small crowd that watched and listened around them.

"We do not lie," the leader held. "We did have knowledge that other Europeans, completely separate from our own faction, were journeying here," he admitted, "but we did not believe that they would attack your people."

The king shook his head in disbelief. "Nonsense," he said.

"The other tribes talked fondly of your people and remarked on the power and skill your people possessed. It would have been unwise to attack you. We saw the display your people made of those intruders on our way over here. Sir, why would we come to you so few in number if our plan was to attack you?" the leader pointed out.

The king thought this over. He looked at the three men. They did not seem threatening, and there were, if his eyes were correct, only three of them.

"Why have you come then?" the king asked.

The men of other looked at each other and then at the king.

"Why have we come here? To make friends, of course! We told you we had befriended your allies, so now we intend to befriend you!"

The leader smiled. He might as well have spat. The king was not touched. "Starting today, we do not have any friends," the king rejected.

A small cheer escaped the crowd.

"We knew befriending you would be difficult, and if you choose to reject our gestures, we will kindly refrain from bothering you again," the leader started.

"Then it is settled. Leave." The king rose from his throne as disappointed grunts were heard in light of the lack of decapitation.

"But," the leader interjected, "we do feel that even though we are not responsible for the deaths of your people, it is entirely within our duty to compensate you."

Slowly, the king returned to sitting. Whispers snaked through the crowd at the sound of the word "compensate."

The king leaned back into his throne and stroked his beard thoughtfully, as he always did when strategy became a requisite.

"We offer you twenty thousand fine bricks for the homes that were destroyed as well as one thousand pounds of grain for the farmlands burned. In addition to this, we offer silk and gold to you, the king," the leader offered.

"So you will pay for the destruction and then leave? So be it," the king accepted.

"Sir," the leader interjected again, "while we will respect your wishes, we must advise that you hear another one of our offers. Your allies spoke of your dislike for a certain tribe, the ones that live on the other half of the island. We have a bid that would prove beneficial for the necessities of our government back in our own lands and serve as an economic and military benefit to you and your people."

Where dismissal had resided in the king's mind, curiosity now took root. And so the men of other explained their bid. They talked about how the island contained multiple resources that they needed, how a committee to survey the island would arrive to inspect certain goods. Lastly they talked about how, in return for his cooperation, materials and weapons would be provided to assist in a potential conquest of the other side of the island. At this part of the bid, his eyes widened, and a primal urge surged through him. This could be his chance to take over what had been theirs ages ago before his birth, back when the eldest elders had walked the earth. It would be his chance to rule wholly over the land as he was meant to. He would be the first king to bring the island, both halves of it, into total bucolic prosperity under the Kialli name. Coaxed by his own acute desires, he accepted, and just like that, he and his people were pulled into the inner workings of an exotic bureaucracy that promised them only what they thought they had deserved from the very beginning.

"What is your name?" the king finally asked after the whole day had been spent working out precise details with his advisers.

"Cobbleton," answered the leader. "William Cobbleton."

Takloh demanded death. Like others in the village, he was displeased with his baba's cooperation with the foreign agenda. He showed his displeasure through silence; for several days, he did not talk to anyone. Nyari also thought any involvement with the foreigners was foolish, although neither one of them had the nerve to voice their opinions openly to the king. Khyik might have been able to accept what the king had agreed to if it had not been for the committee.

The committee, made up of men of other, would survey the island's resources for a year. If these men were not the same as the men who had created the Village of the Twelve Trees, they definitely shared a close resemblance. Khyik always assumed that his baba knew best, but this time he was not so sure. Men different in faction but similar in blood were of the same faction to the untrained eye after all. The men the tribe had now allied with did not look any different from the men who had attacked the island. Khyik knew he was no intellectual, but it did not take one to know that the dead did not like being dishonored. The men of other were not like the islanders in the way they did business. Khyik had been present when they performed various unheard formalities. The men of other had provided the king with a writing tool and bundle after bundle of parchment. William Cobbleton loosely translated what the parchment read; mainly it detailed the agreement, but the king was annoyed by the long monotonous sentences as if someone was trying to explain something to a child that was smart enough to grasp speech but too dimwitted to grasp the concepts.

"In these parts, men agree to something and then shake hands, and that is it," the king complained.

"Yes." William Cobbleton laughed. "I'm afraid our people lack that kind of simplicity. Just a few more things to sign, and it shall be done."

After everything had been signed, the men of other left the village and less than a day later came back with more of themselves. Having allied with the men, the rules of hospitality were now back in place. Granted, the islanders still glared menacingly at any blue or green or amber or gray eyes that met their dark brown ones. The king did throw a small feast for the newcomers out of respect. He could have made it a grand event, but the fact of the matter was that Takloh's deputy naming was set to happen soon, and he did not want to waste his resources on his welcome of the unwelcomed guests.

The actual people who made up the committee were not likable in the eyes of the villagers. It was not solely because they were of other. Rather it was their scrawny stance or the fidgeting of their spectacles that made the islanders feel as if their allied partners were unlike them in the most fundamental ways. The islanders were crystals, little bits of sand made great under immense pressure; they took pride in being products of hardship. The committee members had no scars, no bruises, no stamps of any kind.

The feast was held on the royal verandah. Hardly any village people attended, and many people on the king's chieftain council refused to show up out of protest. The men of other, though generally not disgusted by the islanders' food, did not find themselves captivated by it either. Sometimes their faces would glow at the taste of a fish they had never tried or the juices of a fruit they had never heard of; other times the outlandishness of what they ate would prove overwhelming, and the proof would lie somewhere in their scrunched-up facial expressions.

The committee consisted of fourteen men of other: five geologists, three economists, three servants, and another three men for keeping written records in addition to acting as translators. William Cobbleton was not among the men who were to stay; having spent much of his time in and around the continent of Africa, he was eager to return home. He did, however, attend the feast. A small ship had been prepared for him by his people, and he was set to leave following the closing of the feast. William knew that his superiors would not approve of him leaving his fellow citizens in the hands of savages who claimed good faith. Not wanting to abandon his prospects and leave the well-being of the committee members completely in the hands of the islanders, he had yet another proposal for the king.

The conversation was a lengthy one. The captain of William's departure boat almost set sail without him. When it did end, William was satisfied, and the king was left with a bad feeling in the pit of his stomach, something like starvation even though he had just eaten. In short, William had asked to trade wards to ensure the safety of both parties. The king had refused, but William insisted. He listed all of the practical benefits, even went as far as to promise an education for whichever ward the king chose. Again the king refused. That would have been the end of it were it not for the chiefs who thought having collateral was a good idea. The king offered Olosade, a son of one of the local farmers. William Cobbleton rejected.

"I will be giving you my only son, Samuel. It is only right that you give me someone who holds equally as much weight in your heart," he argued.

"What about Khyik?" one of the chiefs suggested.

The chiefs had become worried over the possibility of having to hand over one of their sons and were quick to jump to Khyik being given as an offering.

"No," the king said flatly.

There was silence; neither the committee members nor the chiefs spoke.

"No. If you are serious in educating him…" He paused.

William Cobbleton nodded his head in confirmation.

"Then I will give you my third born, Anen. He has a thirst for knowledge that Khyik does not possess. Besides, Takloh is needed here, and princesses have no business being learned. If lending you my child will appease whatever formality you people have conjured up, then so be it."

With that being the final agreement, the feast ended. The committee members were shown to the newly constructed huts that had been made solely for them. The king sent one of his servants to fetch Anen. The islanders believed that there were many bonds in a family that were sacred. Among these bonds, none was higher than that of Baba and son.

When Anen came to his baba and heard what was to happen to him, he was speechless. It was like a god casting out its own creation without so much as a second thought. The king looked away when Anen's eyes turned big and bright with tears. He could not look his son in the face as he sentenced him to spend a year away from the only place he had ever called home.

Somewhere along the conversation of his deportation, Anen decided that he was going to put up a fight. It was not a pretty scene; in fact, it had been heartrending. Even William Cobbleton had to look away when Anen resorted to grabbing the king by the ankles. Eventually, the guards came and took him away. Shortly after that, William Cobbleton reassured the king that Anen would be safe before he departed as well. Later the men who oversaw Anen's departure described the ship as being a grand piece of craftsmanship; it was a direct creation from the land of other. It showed that the people, although some factions were harsh, had a vigor about them—the ability to create that which the islanders could only imagine. And so the king felt a little less guilty about what he had done, and he wished his son the best.

VII

SWAHILI: Wavulana Hakuwa
|| ENGLISH: Boys Will Be

Khyik had snuck out of view and was enjoying a swim in the Elder River. Even in the rainy season, with the sun tucked snugly in sheets of clouds, it was unbearably hot, and he had broken the rules to find some relief. In one part of the river, it swelled into a pond-like body of water formed on the Kialli side. It was here that Khyik swam whenever the pressures of princehood outweighed whatever benefits people assumed it had. The fact that he could swim was something to be happy about. It was a skill that very few people in the village had. This was mainly because learning how to swim required one to be at the will of the malicious currents that ran through the river. In the river pond, it was substantially calmer. In spite of this, Khyik still learned to swim by nearly drowning.

It had been a very long time ago, but he remembered it well enough because it was his first time in the water. It had been his first time running away. The day was marked not just in his head but also the heads of everyone who called the island home.

The Day of Burning Breeze they had called it. A heat wave had decided to make its stay, claiming the island as its own as well as a few lives. Instinctively, people on both sides of the island tried to find relief in the Elder River, but many parts of it had dried up, leaving a divisive canyon of dirt in between wary Domka and Kialli eyes. Unwilling even in the face of death to lower themselves to the likes of swine and roll around in mud, the Kialli people had done what they were best at second only to fighting—enduring. Many children Khyik's age had died that day, and the village itself was just recovering from a drought. The onslaught of heat had driven him away from his baba's eye and into the bush, where he could find shade in the shadows of the branches stripped of green.

There, half lost and still too hot for comfort, he stumbled into the river pond, its waters seemingly immune to evaporation. It had been a mock blessing. Khyik had waded out into the water as far as he could and cooled down some when Anen jumped out of nowhere and scared him. Apparently he had been following Khyik, his nosiness not deterred by the heat. Khyik tripped backward and fell away from the shallows and into the deep. It was in his desperate attempt to reach the surface that he gained his skill.

When he surfaced, he found Anen sobbing; apparently he had been down long enough for his older brother to assume the worst had happened. But Anen had inadvertently given him his greatest skill. Anen was also the only other person who knew about the river pond, and through the years, he kept the secret so that Khyik could hide in its mystery. The secrecy made the river pond an Eden for Khyik. He had never thanked Anen for giving him his precious skill or for protecting his only sanctum away from home, but just like with Takloh and Nyari, his love for his sibling did not have to be voiced; it was strong like the current, and that went both ways.

So it was no surprise that when Khyik got back to the village and heard of his brother's departure, he wept. A young boy of other was in the place of where his dear Anen should have been.

Samuel Cobbleton was William Cobbleton's only son. The boy was close to the same age as Khyik, but that was where the similarities ended. Samuel was much shorter than Khyik, short enough that he always had to tilt his head upward just to make eye contact with people he was talking to. Even then, Samuel's orangey-golden hair would get in the way. He would clear his vision by blowing it or by manual adjustment with his hands. Only then could people see his pale-blue irises. Samuel was close to Khyik in age, so the king had thought of no one better than Khyik to help the boy adjust. Khyik had protested, but it was no use.

"He is going through the same thing that Anen is going through right now, so it would be nice if he had the company of someone his own age," the king had said.

Khyik had huffed loudly at the sound of his brother's name.

"Help him," the king ordered. The familiar sting of finality was in his voice.

So the very next morning following the exchange, Khyik got up early and made his way to the guest hut. The boy of other was still asleep, so Khyik waited outside the guest hut.

Other people got up as dawn gave way to day. The translators were first. Most likely, they had to find the village people who would be on the other end of the translated conversations. They would have to find the most knowledgeable farmers to know the land (both its best and worst qualities). They would also find the chiefs to disclose what work would have to be done to the land if, in the future, a full partnership were to occur.

Next to wake up were the servants, then the geologists, and so on. Each man passed Khyik on his way out of the guest hut. They smiled at him courteously enough, but Khyik supposed they only did this because they knew he was the son of the king and not some random village boy. One by one and then a few at a time, the men left the guest hut until there was only one person inside. Khyik grew impatient. His job was to entertain the boy and keep him out of harm's way. This was the exact opposite of what he had in mind at first, which was to bait the boy into a tussle with Takloh—things would have certainly gotten entertaining then. Alas, his plan had been foiled before it could be carried out. No man, Takloh included, would touch Samuel out of diplomacy. It was not just the king who was willing to conform at the promise of the island in completion. The entitled parts of the islanders' hearts swelled at the promise of what was surely destiny. It did not matter much to Khyik; he had it set in his mind to make Samuel miserable.

When Samuel did wake up, Khyik had almost fallen asleep himself. The boy smiled the same as the other people. He wore a peculiar tunic and long pants. The clothing was improper for the island's climate, but Khyik would not care much if heatstroke claimed the boy. Khyik and Samuel looked at each other; each boy sized the other up.

"Hello, sir," Samuel said clumsily.

Khyik suppressed a laugh and nodded before motioning for Samuel to follow him. A translator could not be spared for the two of them, so mostly the boys communicated through gestures. Not knowing what Samuel wanted to see, Khyik wandered aimlessly about the village and pointed when he thought they had come across something noteworthy. He pointed at some fields, a few cattle, the huts of some of the more pristine chiefs, and the kraal. They had not walked for twenty minutes when Samuel stopped. Khyik noticed there was no sound of footsteps behind him, so he turned around. Samuel held his belly and pointed to it.

"You are hungry," Khyik said.

Samuel scratched his head, trying to decipher Khyik's words. Khyik held an imaginary fruit and took a bite from it. Samuel smiled and nodded in confirmation.

Khyik thought of a plan. He motioned for Samuel to follow him. Khyik walked away from whatever lackluster attractions he had been showing and made his way toward the outskirts of the village. When the village stopped and the bush began, he scanned the forestation until he saw a tree with big bright-yellow melons. He turned around to make sure that Samuel was still there. He was, but he was panting, not being able to keep up with Khyik's long strides. Khyik walked to the tree with big yellow melons and reached for one hanging on a low branch. He plucked it, and the branch, relieved from the weight, whisked upward, tossing with it smaller, less lethargic melons all over the floor. Khyik stuck his thumb in his melon to create a hole, and then he held it up to his mouth and squeezed. But he only simulated drinking. He never let the bitter juice touch his lips.

Samuel's stomach growled anxiously as he picked up a melon of his own. He pressed his thumb to it unsuccessfully, and then he tried again. This time a cavity appeared when he took his thumb away. He held the melon up to his face and drank eagerly. It took two seconds total, one second for the juice to actually enter his mouth and one more for the taste to resonate. Samuel flung the melon away, his face contorted as he spat out the flagrant flavor.

Khyik howled with laughter. He did not even care if he got into trouble for his prank; he was just satisfied that it had worked so well. Samuel was not amused. He ran his fingernails along his tongue, trying to scrape away the taste. When he had finally contained his disgust, his shock turned to anger. Samuel rushed at Khyik, and the two boys fell to the ground in a violent tumble. A melon collapsed under their weight, and more gave way with each revolution. Samuel clawed at Khyik, and Khyik clawed back. Punches were thrown and kicks too. Profanities were exchanged, and they would have escalated the conflict even further if the boys had been able to understand one another. Samuel was surprisingly good at fighting, and becoming overpowered, Khyik broke free of Samuel's hold and ran, with Samuel following close behind. Then in one fluid motion, Khyik doubled back and knocked Samuel clear off his legs. It was the one move he had managed to pick up from Takloh. With Samuel scrambling to his feet, Khyik pounced and pinned the boy hard to the ground.

"Damn my baba for trading Anen for you," he whispered.

Samuel struggled to break free but could not. The two boys had wandered quite a ways away from the village in their adrenaline-fueled altercation. Even the trees that surrounded them did not hold melons or other recognizable fruit. Khyik was not sure what he was going to do with Samuel. All he knew was that his brother was gone and that it was somehow Samuel's fault. He tried to calm himself down, but whatever thought process was needed to do so kept being interrupted by the growling of Samuel's stomach, which had now become beastly. Samuel stopped struggling. Khyik wanted to bask in his enemy's surrender, but he sensed something, a trail of air down his neck and the fear that Samuel emitted. Big sharp canine teeth rattled behind his ear. In the corner of his eye, he saw what had been responsible for the growling. Khyik let Samuel go and ever so slowly turned around. He was squatting as he backed away from the creature and Samuel.

It was a wild dog and not one of the smaller, more affectionate ones that village people owned. Its white, black, and brown fur was fuzzy against its slender build, each hair as sharp as each tooth. The dog snarled. Samuel was still on his back, which was no position to face off against such a predator. Knowing this, the wild dog turned its attention to Samuel. Khyik started to turn around to break into a run, but he heard a whimper—not from the dog but from Samuel. A pathetic, tiny little sound that made his helplessness clear. Khyik did not want to think of what his baba might do to him if Samuel were to be eaten, but it was not just that thought alone that kept him from running. The truth was that he had no intention of *killing* Samuel, and running would have been just as good as that. The wild dog took a step closer to Samuel. This single step was enough as the dog loomed over the boy just as Khyik had previously done. Running out of time, Khyik made a quick decision that saved Samuel's life and face. He clapped his hands together, causing the dog to shift its attention back to him. The dog leaped over Samuel and was now just a few feet in front of Khyik. Samuel got to his feet; not knowing which way was the path back to the village, he slowly tiptoed his way to Khyik's side. The two boys looked at each other, and a truce was passed in the glances. Samuel raised up two fists in preparation for a fight. Khyik shook his head as the wild dog inched closer. Its jowls were moist with salivation, and its big yellow eyes were heavy with impulse. He knew enough about wild dogs to know that they often hunted in packs. Even if they did only manage to injure their prey, the commotion of the attack would only bring more killers. Khyik pointed to the wild dog with one finger, and then he held up two, three, and four fingers to explain this to Samuel. Samuel promptly lowered his fist. What ensued next was not coordinated or thought out; it was the only option: panicked running. The boys ran fast, and they ran together.

They could not rely on speed alone. In that area, they were comically outmatched. They did happen to be in a wooded environment, so they used that to their advantage. They turned often and quickly, and although no words could be spoken between heaving breaths, they did work together. When the wild dog started to gain on them, they would split up. Whoever was further ahead would draw the attention of the predator as the other zigzagged past trees and dodged nuisance branches until the other could catch up. They quickly fatigued. Khyik's legs burned, and he tasted blood in his mouth as his overworked heart retaliated. There was more barking off in the distance, and for Khyik, that meant the end of them. When Khyik's legs finally did give out, he was surprised to find that the wild dog was nowhere to be found—and neither was Samuel. Risking more than he wanted to, Khyik got to his aching feet and painfully jogged back toward where he had come from.

"Samuel!" he called.

The boy's name sounded more like "Sam well" when it came out of his mouth, but he was surprised he could say it at all. Just when he suspected the worst had happened to his newly made companion, he caught sight of white arms waving at him. Samuel was propped up against the stump of a tree. At first Khyik feared that he was injured, but closer inspection told him that, just like him, Samuel was only out of breath. Khyik joined Samuel at the tree stump, and both of them said nothing.

Birds chirped in the treetops, trying to drown out the boys' wheezing. After Khyik had regained his breath, he found that they were in a new predicament. They had escaped the wild dog but had become lost in doing so. Samuel did not realize this until he saw that Khyik had not the slightest clue which way the village was. Khyik sighed. At least it was still early; the most dangerous animals came out at night, and once nightfall came, they would be stuck in one spot. Moving around at night was a guaranteed way to become more lost or worse.

Samuel started murmuring inaudibly as he paced around. Khyik could understand why he was agitated. Sure, it was his practical joke that had put them in their predicament in the first place, but he did not see any practicality in arguing. Samuel asked him something, but Khyik could not understand. Instead of spending time trying to figure out what Samuel was asking him, he ignored him and tried to think. This annoyed Samuel, and he paced around, yelling out his agitation. The sun rose in the east. The sour melon trees were on the southern part of the village. They had run away from the village, which meant that they had to go north, but Khyik could not figure out whether they had to go northeast or northwest. The sun had not fully risen yet, so he could not fully use it to his advantage either. After a few more minutes of Samuel's complaining and no sudden decisiveness in his sense of direction, Khyik took a guess and started walking.

Samuel protested but, not wanting to be left behind, followed along before Khyik could disappear out of view. Every now and then, Samuel would say something that Khyik could only assume was unpleasant. Other than that, they both stayed quiet. They walked for a considerably long time until Khyik's hunger forced him to stop. However hungry Khyik was, Samuel was worse off, given that his first meal of the day had been a hoax. Khyik patted his belly. Samuel in turn rolled his eyes. Khyik looked around for anything edible. He was surrounded by plenty of berries, but he had not spent enough time in the bush to know which ones were safe to eat. Not wanting to take a gamble on his life, he searched for something he was sure was safe. A quick glance at the sky showed a tessellation of leaves; the sun was somewhere behind the canopy. Their hunger was pinching, and they could not go very long without having one of their stomachs groan. Khyik had almost given up when he found a pile of grass seeds under a bush. They were bland and would not keep them full for long, but they were safe and plentiful.

Samuel had been more reluctant to put the brown bunches in his mouth. He knew better than to pick berries at random, especially if Khyik was not eating them. He had been going to pass on the forest snack altogether until his stomach gave one last growl in protest. The grass-seed bunches were not tasty treats; they had a bland, nutty flavor that was dwarfed by a grassy aftertaste. Still there was plenty to go around, so the boys ate their fill. When they finished, they resumed walking.

The sound of water was what told Khyik that they had gone the wrong way. Fortunately, Samuel did not catch on, which was a good thing because Khyik had no desire to hear more of his complaints. Khyik ran toward the water, and he came to find the Elder River. Its waters were chugging along, oblivious to the boys' struggle. He made his way down to the riverbank, kneeled down, and cupped his hands to scoop up a sample of water. Samuel also quenched his thirst; he was happy to find a source of water, but he would have much rather found the village. Although they had been going the wrong way, finding the river was a good sign. It would lead them to more familiar places that would allow Khyik to trace the village.

As they walked, Samuel said something that Khyik could not understand. From the upward inflection, it resembled a question. Samuel held out his hand and made a walking animation with two fingers.

"Ahh," Khyik said understandingly.

Samuel wanted to know where they were going. He thought for a moment. There was no easy way to explain adequately by motions. Khyik grabbed a long stick on the ground to Samuel's alarm. He had no intention of using it as a weapon though. He found a soft spot on the bank and started to draw. Samuel was amused, and he watched inquisitively. Khyik drew a cluster of huts and then drew two long squiggly lines adjacent to one another to symbolize the river. The river ran alongside the cluster of huts. Finally, Khyik drew two crude figures, one with bushy hair and another with wild straight locks.

Samuel laughed and nodded. Khyik put the stick down, and the two of them continued on their way.

Khyik never formally apologized for what he did to Samuel; nevertheless, they became friends that day. By the time they eventually did find the village, they had shared numerous conversations almost entirely without talking. Khyik had pointed out some of the local wildlife and even taught Samuel to say a few phrases in the Kialli language. Samuel had in return taught Khyik phrases in the language of other. The two of them shared similarities that neither suspected existed, primarily their ability to find trouble. Nyari greeted them when they got back. It was not a greeting per se as much as it was a scolding with two recipients.

"Where have you two been?" she asked.

"We got chased by a wild dog and got lost in the bush," Khyik explained.

"Why were you near wild dogs?" Nyari asked. The answer had not appeased her.

"Melons," Samuel said suddenly.

"Melons?" Nyari repeated.

The two boys laughed, and Khyik disregarded his sister's scolding. Samuel ate with the men of other when he reached the guest huts. Khyik said good-bye and went to have a meal of his own in the kraal. When Khyik got to the kraal, he found Takloh waiting on the verandah. Takloh was cleaning one of his blades.

"We almost had to have a search party go out and look for you," he said before Khyik entered.

"Ah, I am sorry, brother. We got lost and—"

Takloh held up his hand.

"We thought he had murdered you," Takloh said bluntly.

"We do not trust these people, which means you do not trust these people. I managed to calm Baba down easily enough, but you should have seen him. He was ready to go through every one of them. I am not a friend of these people, but I did not want that to happen. Even if I did want it to, I must consider what would become of Anen. You would be wise not to let this happen again," Takloh warned.

Khyik knew he had been reckless.

"Yes, brother," he said.

VIII

FRANÇAIS: C'est La Vie
|| ENGLISH: It Is Life

A man the men of other called Paul Leonard was the head geologist. He was the man who did most of the work regarding determining the usefulness of the island's resources. Paul Leonard routinely had the king talk him through some of the more unknown secrets of the island—an animal that his education in biology could not name or a plant that had some obscure importance. On one of these visits, the king asked Khyik to join him. Paul Leonard, the king, and Khyik, along with some translators and two chiefs, met on one of the village's biggest farms.

Paul Leonard was a masculine fellow unlike the majority of his co-workers. The man had bulging biceps and a thick beard that rivaled the king's. He did wear dainty spectacles, but they were so easily forgotten on the man's large and commanding face. Paul Leonard wanted to see what was grown locally. At the start of their study, the men of other had spent so much of their time looking for the island's more exotic attributes that they did not take the time to look at the more common things. Paul Leonard's wavy black hair was tucked behind his ears on either side. He held a parchment, which sat on a hardwood board.

"And this, I assume it's cassava?" he asked through a translator.

"Yes, yes," the king responded. "It grows abundantly here," he bragged.

"It grows abundantly in many of the lands on this side of the world," Paul Leonard pointed out to the king's slight irritation.

"That is true. It hardly needs help from a farmer to grow well," the king admitted. "You did say that you wanted to focus on the more common things today, didn't you?"

Paul Leonard sighed. "Yes, I suppose I did."

"Well then, if cassava is too common, we have other things. How useful are, say, bananas or mangoes?" the king asked.

"The mangoes might be worth a look," said Paul Leonard.

The king led the way with the men and Khyik following closely behind. The king pointed to a series of trees each bestrewed with bright, bulging round fruit.

"Have you a ladder?" Paul Leonard asked.

The king smiled, and with one quick motion, he jumped with his arms outstretched and grabbed a not-so-low branch. He effortlessly pulled himself up onto it and plucked several of the mangoes from the tree. When he had plucked a few dozen, he jumped down.

"You should have allowed me to do it," said one of the chiefs.

"Nonsense," replied the king. "I need to show these men that I can handle my own island."

Paul Leonard picked up a mango and studied it. He jotted down several notes and even made a few quick sketches. Khyik helped himself to one. He could not fathom why giving a fruit so much attention was necessary. He took a bite of the mango in his palm.

"Pay attention!" the king snapped.

Khyik dropped the fruit and proceeded to listen to the translator ramble on as Paul Leonard rambled on about the mangoes.

"These are very good mangoes," Paul Leonard concluded.

Khyik sighed. One could have known that just by looking at them.

"The soil is good too. How much rainfall does this area get?" Paul Leonard asked.

"Enough to reach a man's knees in the rainy season," the king answered.

Paul Leonard scribbled down some more notes. Khyik found the rest of that evening unbearably boring. Paul Leonard would ask some unsurprising, almost predictable question and the king or a chief would give the answer. Paul Leonard would then study the item as his hand whisked across his notebook. When everything had concluded and Khyik was allowed to excuse himself, he was ecstatic and hid it poorly.

"Next time at least pretend to take some interest. These are matters of the island after all," the king scolded.

Khyik went to go meet up with Samuel, who had been waiting patiently on the other side of the village next to the sour melon trees.

"Why so long?" Samuel asked.

"The one you call Paul Leonard," Khyik explained.

"Oh" was all Samuel replied. He understood the man's particular tendencies when it came to his work.

Khyik had learned a little of the language of other and practiced words in his head as he looked up into the sky. The stars could be seen clearly that night. Since Khyik had made a point of learning the language of other, it had not been nearly as difficult as he thought it would be. In just a few short weeks, he had gone from knowing next to nothing to being able to hold short conversations in the tongue. The boys had grown very close in that time. At the start of their unlikely friendship, they were not able to talk much, but as soon as they could, they talked about everything there was to talk about. They talked about their families, for one. Khyik had learned that Samuel's life was surprisingly full of adversities. Khyik had asked why Samuel had not looked upset when his baba traded him as a ward. He knew it was personal, but curiosity got the best of him; it slipped out of his mouth before he could stop himself. Samuel had been a little taken aback, but he did answer. Despite what people thought, William Cobbleton was not Samuel's baba.

Some Time Ago in the Land of Sam...

Brittany Osher had been the daughter of a wealthy real-estate tycoon who sold top-tier properties in London. She had been a quiet woman, never drawing much attention to herself. She never advertised her need for love, so all her suitors had to do the extra work of advertising theirs; there was no middle point to meet at. Brittany would have to run her father's company someday, and she would have to do so completely behind closed doors. If it had been made public that the company was being run by a woman, the business partners would have all fled. Some day, she would have to be the ultimate puppet master, a solitary mastermind to a valuable empire. It was this empire's value that took priority over her need for love.

But in all her years, her heart had never leaped for someone as it leaped for a poor cobbler named Gabriel Harrington, who owned a little shop next to her father's building. The man was gruff and hard on her eyes as well as her heart; that was what she had loved most about him. Her father, Douglas, had been a frugal man and often asked her to take his old overused shoes to be fixed at Gabriel's tiny shop. Gabriel had made quite an impression on her. Perhaps it was his own disinterest, his own complete engagement in his work that left no room for love that attracted her to him. She was a bee, and he was a flower, spilling at the beams with nectar. It was unfortunate that in the end her adventurous wings burned.

William Cobbleton had been a business partner of her father. Their relationship had grown deep over the years, as they did lots of work together. Brittany was independent and liked being in complete control of herself, and her father knew this, so she was caught off guard when he confronted her and told her to marry William. He used her future control of the company as leverage and threatened to name William as a business partner. Her father did not know of her attraction to Gabriel, but William did. Through subliminal persuasion, he convinced Brittany's father to pay off the landlords and buy Gabriel's shop since the man would never give up his shop willingly. The company used the surplus square footage as an addition to their building, and Gabriel was kicked out.

With Gabriel gone and William becoming more favorable by the day, she decided to give in and marry him. He was a sensible option, and she thought she could bear it, but she had not anticipated the foulness of William's personality. It disgusted her, but as her father grew older and sickly, it was the only thing that brought a smile to his face, his apprentice and his daughter bound together by a love that he had no desire to know was faux. When her father did die, she gained control of the company and even attempted to divorce her husband, but William was an immortal pest. She did not have the power to divorce her husband alone, not without male support to back her claims of her husband's ill will toward her.

By pure chance, she found Gabriel, and they started an affair. He offered to help her divorce William, and for a while, they were happy. That is until William found out. He was a man with many ties to many different people, some of them with darker souls than even he had, people who were willing to do the dirtiest of dirty work for the right price. She had read it in the paper under the obituaries. William had only watched. He heard her cries along with the shattering of her teacup, but he could not bring himself to care.

A deep pain lingered in her bosom from that day on. She was pregnant with Gabriel's baby, a son. She knew it was Gabriel's child, and the thought of caring for a product of their love gave her hope that she could once again find happiness. But the saddest story started off hardly happy and only got worse. She died during childbirth, leaving the company she had worked her entire life for in the hands of a man she did not love. Also, in his hands was Samuel, her only child. William Cobbleton knew the moment he held Samuel that the child was not his. He gave Samuel to an orphanage multiple times. He would drop him off, leave, change his mind, and then pick him up again. William Cobbleton had hated his wife, but only because she had tortured him with unrequited love. He only hated her because she would not give him the only thing that he had ever wanted from her. Every man had some kind of boundary; even the most ruthless men abided by some equally ruthless code. William's code would not allow him to give up Samuel. Samuel had been the last thing that she loved, and he had Samuel, so in a way he did have her love in the end.

William sold off the company in favor of a more nomadic lifestyle as an explorer and merchant. He took Samuel under his wing...under his iron fist. It was a hard life under William's tutelage, but it could have been worse. Samuel only learned of his origins through one of his mother's friends, who had preferred to be nameless, upon meeting him by chance at a market and telling him his story. William was not a father as much as he was a supervisor, and Samuel treated him as such. Samuel had the same trait as his mother in that he could not bring himself to love William, but, strangely, he could not bring himself to hate him either.

When Khyik heard this story, he felt sadness for his friend. Samuel insisted that he had accepted what had happened and that most of the time he was content with the way he lived.

"So you will not avenge your baba?" Khyik asked, baffled by Samuel's calm.

Samuel seemed to think it over in his head.

"Maybe someday, but I would have to be tactful about it. For right now, I rely on him for too much."

Khyik advised Samuel not to tell anyone else of the story. "My baba exchanged Anen on the basis that you were William's son. Were he to find out that was not the case, he would be very, very displeased," Khyik said as an understatement.

"I would not dream of telling your father," Samuel said.

The two boys now watched the stars shine in the sky. It was a usual occurrence, but that night the stars felt just a little brighter and their twinkles just a little clearer.

"Tell me," Samuel started, "does your father hate my kind?"

Khyik was not expecting a heavy question.

"No," he answered. "But he hates what they've done, what some of them are doing, I mean. I could be wrong; I often am, but I do not think he hates your people."

Khyik patted Samuel on his back and went to the kraal to sleep.

IX

LINGALA: Boból̵o ||
ENGLISH: Friendship

Samuel enjoyed many things on the island. He enjoyed the weather because it was less gloomy than the seemingly permanent sheet of gray that occupied the skies of London. He enjoyed the food, even if it did not sit well in his stomach sometimes. He enjoyed the animals. He enjoyed the zeal people had for living everyday life.

Added on to the list of things he enjoyed was Nyari. He enjoyed her company; she corrected him often as he tried to learn to speak Kialli. She even corrected his English when he misphrased a sentence. With a machine of a mind, a mind capable of originality beyond what was thought possible for simple island people, she produced beautiful artwork. She had been throwing out some of her paintings one day. A pile of neatly stacked thin wood boards decorated with color was in the middle of the kraal's compound. Khyik and Samuel had been on their way to skip smooth stones on the river when they came across it. Khyik did not give much thought to the collection that his sister was throwing away. She frequently deplenished and replenished her stock of personal artwork. Samuel, on the other hand, had been mesmerized by every stroke of color, the tricky collage of a zebra's stripes, the thin brown legs of an impala on the plains, and the off-putting eyes of a predator lurking behind green cover. Everything she painted seemed to come to life. Samuel had stopped immediately. He started going through each wooden slice of life, piece by wonderful piece. Nyari came out of the kraal, her arms stacked high with more of her unneeded works of art.

"These are beautiful!" Samuel complimented.

She walked over to her now not-so-neat pile and dropped off her most recent load.

"Thank you." She smiled.

"Yes, they are very well done," Khyik chimed in.

"You have never been one to compliment my work before," Nyari said, her eyelids coming together in an accusing squint.

Samuel took his eyes from the art and looked at Khyik in disapproval.

"Well, everyone under the sun knows that your artwork is the best," Khyik said, reinforcing his praise.

"A compliment from you is nice to hear." She smiled from ear to ear and knelt down to join Samuel.

The two chatted about her various depictions of life on the island. Khyik was annoyed; he had been looking forward to showing off his stone-skipping skills, and now he would not get to. He was going to try to separate Samuel from the paintings, but he realized his efforts would be futile when his words went unnoticed by the two of them. Not wanting to be left out, Khyik knelt down and joined them. He had always known his sister was an amazing artist—the best on the island—but he had never inquired about her work very deeply. He did not know that she had a routine for painting. He did not know how she got the colors to become so vivid or the techniques she used. For most of the morning, they went through each painting, and for every one they went through, Nyari would throw in a new fact. By the time they were done,

Khyik had gained a new level of appreciation for his sister's talents, Samuel had gained another thing to like on the island, and Nyari had lost her desire to get rid of her old artwork.

"But where will I find room for them all?" she said to herself.

"We could always make a collage," Samuel suggested.

Nyari and Khyik looked at each other with perplexed faces. Catching on that they did not follow, Samuel explained what a collage was. When he finished his explanation, both Khyik and Nyari thought it was a fine idea.

"We will need to find a place to put it," Khyik pointed out.

The three of them thought silently.

"How about the side of the kraal?" Samuel suggested. "It has more than enough space."

Khyik and Nyari were unsure.

"I do not know if Baba would allow it," Nyari said.

"He would not," Khyik said bluntly. "But what about the tree? The one that Baba's outdoor throne is under."

"The bush willow?" Nyari asked.

Khyik nodded.

The three of them walked over to the large tree. Its branches were elongated and spindly, but the body was round and wide, fit enough to host their collage. They wasted no time in getting to work. Khyik found a servant and requested for the stickiest batch of tree sap available, and a bowl of it was fetched. It had been unused for quite some time but was far from going stale. Adhesive juice from the inside of an African evergreen would serve well. Nyari organized the paintings; she told the two boys where everything should go. Samuel went inside the kraal and came back with a thick horsehair brush. He dipped it in the sap and slathered the backs of the boards before placing them exactly where Nyari instructed. When they had finished, the base of the bush willow was elaborately covered with Nyari's old paintings. They admired their handiwork.

It was not long before the king caught word of what was being done to his tree, and he initially came out to scold them, but when he saw how well placed everything was and how well it fit the wood, all animosity left him.

"You have your mother's eye for decoration," he said.

The three of them turned around.

"It looks mighty fine," he complimented. "Very bright of you to do it."

Nyari smiled again.

"It was Samuel's idea, Baba," Khyik said.

The king looked surprised. "Is this true?"

"Yes, sir," Samuel confirmed.

The king had made a habit of not talking to his ward. He was not comfortable with all of his own children let alone the child of someone else, and he had no desire to converse. His only responsibility was keeping the boy safe.

"Well, that was a fine idea," he said to Samuel.

Samuel smiled the way Nyari had. The collage was admirable. Each frame looked ten times as beautiful as the last. It was a small thing, but the king was impressed by Samuel, if only a little more than before.

In the middle of the night, Takloh woke up Khyik. Khyik wondered what was going on, but Takloh allowed no time for explanation.

"Meet me out in front of the kraal!" Takloh ordered.

Khyik got up groggily and followed his brother's shadow out to the front of the kraal and under the moonlight.

"What are we doing?" Khyik asked.

"It is not a matter of what we are doing but of where we are going," Takloh replied.

"Well, then, where are we going?" Khyik asked, annoyed.

Takloh did not answer. Instead, he started off in a direction, and Khyik reluctantly followed behind. They were walking south and would soon be exiting the village.

"Wait!" Khyik called suddenly.

Takloh came to a slow stop. "What is it? I told you, just follow me."

"Can we bring someone else along?" Khyik asked.

Takloh looked confused. "There is no one else who will find where we are going useful."

"What about Samuel?" Khyik asked hopefully.

"No," Takloh answered.

"Why? You said yourself no one will find where we are going useful. Even if it is interesting, Samuel will not tell anyone," Khyik pleaded.

Takloh thought this over. His eyes rolled, and Khyik knew that he had been swayed.

"Bring him quickly!" said Takloh as Khyik ran into the guest hut.

He entered in a hurry, almost tripping over several sleeping people. Luckily, Samuel was not very far into the hut. Khyik shook him vigorously with both hands until a glob of drool dripped from his mouth and his eyelids parted.

"What? What is it?" Samuel asked, rubbing his crusty eyes.

"Follow me. We are going on an adventure," Khyik said.

Khyik walked out of the guest hut and made his way back to Takloh. He was unsure as to whether Samuel had followed him, but sure enough, the boy emerged from the darkness.

"Stay with us" was all Takloh said before he started running into the bush.

Khyik followed closely behind, as did Samuel. They were both sleepy, but the thrill of sneaking off in the night sent adrenaline straight through their veins. The moonlight kept the floor of the bush well lit enough so that they could avoid its obstacles—a thornbush, a snake curled up in slumber, a sharp cone…they dodged it all. Samuel was faster than Khyik had expected. Multiple times Samuel almost overtook him, but not wanting to look slow in front of his brother, Khyik would adjust his speed and stay a stride or two ahead. Takloh would not have even seen if Samuel had gone faster than Khyik anyway; it was dimly lit, and he was too far ahead, his powerful legs launching him into the night. Eventually, they came to a clearing where sandy shores and a canoe propped up against a hump in the land waited for them.

"Get in. Khyik, you take the other oar. We will alternate," Takloh instructed.

The three of them got in, and Khyik took the oar just as he was told. The adrenaline must have increased because Khyik felt more energized than ever before. The cold water against his feet had made him wide awake. He paddled vigorously, switching sides whenever Takloh had finished paddling. Samuel sat in the canoe and observed the moon's reflection in the calm waters. Khyik wanted to ask where they were going, but he was too involved in paddling. In the distance was a little formation of land, a very tiny little thing, but it had enough mass to peek over the water. Within minutes, they were upon it. It was a miniature island; the circumference of the land could be traveled in one tedious jog if they had wanted to run around it.

"What is this place?" Samuel asked as he unsteadily got out of the canoe, almost falling into the water.

"This is my home away from home," Takloh answered.

Khyik had only taken a few dozen steps, and already he was in the center of the island. There was a sand dune that acted as a hill from where he could see everything on the horizon that surrounded them. The island—the bigger one that they called home—was just a little ways away.

"Most nights the sea mist covers this little piece of land, so it is mostly invisible," Takloh explained.

Samuel had gotten curious, and he met Takloh at the top of the sand dune. The sand was cool, and it stuck to their moist feet.

"This is amazing!" Samuel exclaimed.

Takloh smiled at Samuel's liking of his place, "Yes, it is. I would appreciate it if you could keep it a secret."

"Of course," Samuel said, nodding his head. "Of course."

Besides a few small trees and a few larger ones that had fallen and made a wooden obstacle course on the sand, there was very little on the island.

"Ah! I have something for us!" Takloh said.

He walked over to a slight lump in the ground. He knelt down and started digging. He pulled up a large gourd with a cork in the opening. He brought it to his mouth, wrapped his teeth around the cork, and pulled. He spit out the cork along with bits of sand.

"I will be named deputy soon. The duties of being king will be passed to me when Baba passes. I will be busy in the midst of men and chiefs when the day arrives, so I wanted to celebrate early with you, brother, in case I do not have an opportunity in the future," Takloh said.

Samuel looked down, feeling awkward because he was intruding on the moment.

"You as well, friend of my brother," Takloh added.

Khyik and Samuel walked to Takloh and took turns in drinking palm wine from the gourd. The unexpected taste of it, appropriate for the unexpected night, was surprisingly sweet. Khyik and Samuel had finished half of the gourd when Takloh took it from them and took one hefty swig.

"You two drink like women," he teased.

The three of them laughed. They spent a long time just enjoying the sight—the sheet of silver cast on the surface of the water by the moon, the white sand, the clear black sky dotted with white diamonds...it was all so beautiful.

"We should head back now," Takloh said after a while.

Khyik and Samuel did not want to leave, but they forced their feet off the island and back into the canoe. This time Samuel took the oar, and Khyik sat down. He felt like telling his brother about his own hideout, his home away from home, but the only reason Takloh had revealed the secret island was because there was a special occasion happening. Khyik decided that when and if there was such an occasion for him, he would take Takloh to the river pond.

When they got back to the village, they each went back to their respective sleeping places without saying a word to each other, but a very loose bond had been created between the three of them. It was based on a single secret trip, and although it was not at all strong, it was there.

X

IGBO: N'agbụ Ka Nwatakịrị ‖ ENGLISH: Chains for a Child

After much ado, the day finally came that Takloh would be named deputy. All of the villagers and even the committee were excited. It had been delayed multiple times, so when the day finally came, there was an expectation that the festivities would be carried out quickly before anything else could further postpone them. Goats that had been saved were brought out and slaughtered. The village men skinned the bodies, and the village women prepared the meat. The committee, having not seen a true celebration except for the feast on the day of their arrival, which had been colorless in every way, were also eager. They put off their work and helped the men of the village build the required decorative trinkets. Some even helped the servants set up long tables of food around the compound of the royal kraal. Important people from all of the Kialli villages arrived throughout the day; some of them Khyik had never heard of before.

A contagious buzz was in the air. The festive zest even reached Takloh, who was the center of attention. Normally expressionless, every inch of him moved with a renewed vitality that neither the king nor the Kialli people had seen since he was very young. Any severity in the village people dissipated that day, leaving nothing but unadulterated joy. Torches with handles that the village woodworkers had custom-carved were lit as soon as it got dark. The flames and their finely crafted handles were placed all around. In the final act of celebratory preparation, drums were brought out, and a foot-tapping beat echoed in the night at the collision of open palms against drum heads. The royal kraal, which was normally open and spacious, had become crowded and cozy. When the king produced the traditional deputy headdress, the garnish of multicolored feathers on it flapped about as if they were still attached to live birds. The cause of their animation could only be attributed to the smiling faces and moving feet and bellies being made full by the minute; waves were being made by the lives that gathered in the night, and those waves gave the feathers flight.

As the king was placing the headdress on Takloh's head and the wildness of the feast was reaching its peak, there was a confidential anniversary that had been forgotten. Unbeknownst to the villagers, an undead member of their kinfolk was making his way toward them. That day was also the anniversary of the day that the Domka had kidnapped Orlo, the king's second born.

It was often said by the Kialli that the dead did not like being disrespected. Little did they know that the saying applied even when the dead were not truly dead. At that very moment, a forgotten son was on his way back, ready to make himself known once again. When the Domka had taken the king's second born long ago, it had been in a rushed attack that had ended as quickly as it had begun.

Orlo had been much quieter than Takloh. He did not seek attention from his mother nearly as often, so even though Takloh was no longer an only child, much of the attention still remained on him and not his new little brother. No one remembered exactly how old Orlo had been when he was kidnapped, but it was around the time that most young ones start voicing the titles Mamma and Baba.

The king was just returning from a hunt, and the queen was walking around the village with her most recent son in her clutches. She had put him down only for a moment to dry her palms when a small band of Domka men emerged from the bush and snatched the boy. The boy had screamed, the queen had cried out for her son, and the king had been too slow to round up his men. They ran after what was already lost. There was an informal funeral for him; everyone assumed the Domka had killed the boy. The king and queen prayed that it was a quick death, they had a procession where all the chiefs were present to sympathize, and then it was over. He became nothing more than a memory. But rarely did a memory remember.

Chains for a Child...

Scary faces with disingenuous smiles covering yellow teeth that revealed intentions that were yellower still—these were the things that Orlo remembered. Contrary to what the Kialli side of the island thought, the Domka men did not kill him. He had been passed around like an obese pipe among lazy countrymen, switching hands from handler to handler, salesman to salesman, until he met the open shackle of a white man on a big boat. Orlo filled that shackle for the price of a sack of gold and additional tobacco to fill the pipe.

The white man he was sold to was nice enough for a slaver. He did not mutilate any of the slaves on board as other similar slavers had done when the victims would get too rowdy. He even took the shackles off Orlo every once in a while, but it did little good. A child could not play when he was seasick. The crew that drove the boat onward to Orlo's fate was not as kind as the captain, and a slave child running amok would only anger them. They complained often and told the captain that showing a little grace to the savage boy would only cause trouble. The captain heeded this and kept Orlo's unsupervised wandering to a minimum. For the few times that the shackles did come off, Orlo stayed close to the captain where it was safe. The crew members twisted his ears till they throbbed, when the captain was not watching. If the captain dozed off and he ran into one on a particularly bad day, he was sure to get a beating. The captain was his cage as much as the ship was; he held him in but kept other things out. He wore a large overcoat that could have been made out of several dozens of the loincloths that the slaves wore. Orlo could not understand how a man could wear such clothing when the heat hit the sails with as much indiscriminate ferocity as the men who positioned them.

The ride to the new world had been fun in comparison with the new world itself. At least on the boat, sprinkles of sparkling saltwater broke his attention away from his endless fear instead of the prickly end of a whip. On the boat, he had the captain's pet to gaze at, which was a sly flightless jackdaw. The bird had been everything but friendly. It had hissed at him, and he found himself covered in its goopy off-white excrement often, but it too was a slave. Its silvery-blue hue was never as vibrant as the white of the gulls that flew above the towering masts. Those free birds sang the chantey of their unimpeded existence, and the spiteful jackdaw had heckled profoundly whenever an outstretched white wing cast a shadow over its beak. No, the captain's bird was not Orlo's friend, but Orlo had been its friend until the very end. He had fed it whatever was left over from his daily meal of hard bread. He had done his best to shoo off any crew members who bothered the bird (even though it often resulted in a beating for him). He even went as far as to sing to it verses of village songs he was finding increasingly difficult to remember. He was its friend until the day the ship was no longer his home.

Going through the auctions, he could not, in all honesty, call the ship brutal, and if he did, then the auctions were several tiers higher in brutality. While being auctioned off, he watched as families were split apart like logs. While it was true he had been taken from his family, that did not hurt as heavily as did the sight of the same crime done to others.

Orlo was sold to a plantation owner by the name of Mr. Loring, who, according to the mouths of slaves and plantation owners alike, was one of the harshest men in the South. This was true. His many fields were lined with horrendous magnolias ornamented with the skulls of servants who could not survive a blow from his iron fist. Even children's skulls banged against the dreadful bark. Mr. Loring's trees were famous; they were the ones with harlequin skeletons swaying like chimes on the branches. Screams could be found somewhere deep in the roots, but evidently they could not reach the eardrums of Mr. Loring. Where others heard suffering, he heard money; where others saw murder, he saw failed investments. He had one of the most successful plantations in his area. The jewel of his plantation was a big, white, fully staffed mansion. If one were to approach the house, the first thing one would see was a framed sign hung on the door that read, "As for me and my house, we will serve the Lord—Joshua 24:15."

In Mr. Loring's eyes, his estate was a pious place and not the neoclassical dungeon that others saw it to be. It was the sacrosanct dwelling of a self-proclaimed saint. His wielding of the whip was the will of the Almighty, and although he might have claimed to serve God, his home was no hospice. His house was not one that was under the Lord's control but one that was under his. His own leisure and projected fascism made him Jehovah and every potentially equal man his servant.

"The biggest bundles of money cannot be earned without blood. Theirs fall because it has to; mine falls because I grip the whip hard," Mr. Loring would say to his associates.

Whippings were daily, even on Sundays when a lot of other plantation owners would take the day off. Not Mr. Loring though. Every morning he would find the slaves who had picked the least from the day before, call all the other slaves to watch, and whip them until the ridges of their spines were barely covered by skin. Twice Orlo found himself subjected to the treatment, once when he was only thirteen and another time a few years later. Both times, he had almost died. Many did but not him. He went on to become the top picker on the plantation. The calluses on his hands had become so hard that they shielded him from most herbal barbs, and even when they failed, he was devoid of pain because the whippings had damaged his nerves.

Orlo's life was one full of confusion, sweat, obedience, and subordination. Every morning, he would feed the swine their slop, and then immediately after, he would head for the fields equipped with only a canteen of water and a bit of moonshine. There he would systematically go down the rows of cotton until he looked up and could no longer see the sun. The fields had a few overseers on staff, but none of them ever bothered Orlo. They knew he was the plantation's best picker and that whipping him would only slow him down. When Orlo was finished, he would head back to his shack. Since he was the top picker, Mr. Loring had rewarded him with his own shack. It was not much, but Orlo appreciated his privacy. He never socialized with the other slaves because he did not consider himself a slave, at least not mentally. In his head, he was the son of a king. Orlo was fixated only on rejoining his tribe; this was his only concern. This was until he met Lilah Dupree, a young slave woman he was to impregnate by the order of Mr. Loring. He had no interest in her. She was four or five years older than him, and she was a gardener. Most of the slaves spat the word "gardener" out to show their disapproval, mainly in its sweetness compared with their bitter title of "field hand."

Lilah was light skinned, which usually warranted indoor work, but her plantation had had an abundance of light-skinned slaves, so they put her outside to garden, which was still a far cry from field labor. So when

Orlo came back to his shack after a day of field work and found Lilah sitting on his bed, he had no idea what to do with her. For one week, she stayed in his shack, and for one week, he ignored her. Eventually, Mr. Loring confronted Orlo regarding his refusal. He had her fetched from Orlo's shack and stripped down naked, and then he bound her by her wrists to a baby conifer. She cried helplessly as he whipped her, forcing her closer to the needles of the tree. He whipped her six times and was readying his arm for the seventh when Orlo reluctantly gave in; he was not a heartless man. Mr. Loring would not be fooled, and wanting to humiliate his best worker as punishment, he had a house slave fetch him a chair. Orlo would copulate with her under the watchful, unapologetic eye of Mr. Loring.

"Get on with it, nigger!" he called. He had a pint of beer in one hand. The other was dangling over a curled whip propped up against his chair.

Orlo knelt down behind her. She sobbed into the tree, not caring anymore about the needles picking at her face; whatever pain came from them was minute. The blood was already starting to dry on her wounds. Orlo slowly grabbed the small of her back, careful not to touch her where it would hurt. He was not erect but did not want to fathom what Mr. Loring would do if he did not impregnate her right then and there. So he yanked on his manhood until it gained some life. He looked at Mr. Loring, who only drank, looked back, and moved his hand closer to the whip. Realizing then that there was no way to avoid it, Orlo squeamishly injected himself. There was no pleasure in the deed. Every time he slowed, Mr. Loring would reach for his whip. He even went as far as to call on the other slaves and make them watch. He made them watch even after he, having grown bored of it, went inside.

"Don't stop fucking that heifer till I tell you, boy; otherwise, it'll be the last thing you do."

When Mr. Loring was satisfied with the longevity of the sex, he reappeared outside and told Orlo to stop. Orlo was sore by then. Lilah did not fare much better; she was bruised. He felt sorry for her, felt sorry that she would have to suffer again in a matter of months delivering a child that no one but the devil wanted.

She never did deliver that child. A few weeks after the event, it was discovered that Lilah Dupree was barren. Orlo did not know that Mr. Loring had bought her for a hefty sum and that her previous owners had refused to refund Mr. Loring's money for selling him a sterile slave. One day, just like any other, Orlo was out in the fields working when a fellow slave pointed at two figures on a hillock just beyond them. The hillock was an unofficial overseer; it gained no pay, but it watched the fields even after the workers left, always. It had no trees or bushes or flowers. It was just a virgin slope of land that never had anyone on it. But that day was different. Orlo watched as one figure pushed the other figure up to the top of the hillock. Then without warning, the one figure doing all the pushing pulled out a cocked pistol and ended the life of the other. It was only when the gunshot rang out past the rows of cotton that Orlo recognized the figures as Mr. Loring and poor Lilah Dupree. The slaves working in the field looked at them for a short time before the overseers put them back to work with whips. Orlo had resumed working quicker than anyone else; he wanted no one to think he had emotionally invested in the poor girl, but the truth was that he was deeply bothered.

That night when he got into his shack, he soaked his feet in warm water and reflected. He could not say that he loved the woman, but he certainly could not say that she deserved to be shot point-blank for the simple, unavoidable crime of not being able to bear a child that neither he nor she wanted. He tried to sleep, but every time he closed his eyes, all he could see was the limp figure on the hillock. She would remain there for all to see until the worms ate away at her flesh, until the flies picked her bones clean, until the bones were carried off by scavengers, and until the hillock appeared to be the same as if nothing had ever happened.

That was when Orlo decided that he needed to escape, not when she had died quickly, but while he had watched her body decay slowly, day after day. If she could not have children, it did not change the fact that she herself had been someone's child, someone's daughter, and there she was just decomposing. She had died as property. Compost. He would not die that way. He wanted to escape. He wanted to escape the lash that left lasting scars. He wanted to escape Sunday mornings, when a cock's call at daybreak and compulsory hymns, sung by the hoarse voices of an overburdened choir, signaled another day of back-breaking work. He wanted to escape into a life where believing in a god would not be a facetious diversion. He might sing hallelujah all on his own if only he could be free. He needed to go home before he forgot what home was. He had saved up more than enough money to buy his way to freedom, but he knew that Mr. Loring would sooner die than see his best slave go free, so that was what needed to happen.

Every night the overseers would do their rounds to make sure things were where they were supposed to be before reporting to Mr. Loring on the house porch for their pay. Orlo waited until the next night for an overseer to walk by his shack. When the man was in ear-shot, he smashed some pieces of scrap metal together that he had collected from the fields. The man stopped.

"What's going on in there?" he called.

Orlo peeked through the crack of his door. The man was holding an oil lamp, his other hand next to a whip hanging off his belt. Orlo made some more ruckus, and the overseer was lured. He drew his weapon. The overseer took two steps into his shack. Orlo quickly clasped his hand around the man's mouth and stabbed him twice in the back; only when the man stopped twitching did he let go. The man fell to the floor, and blood trickled out of him from his sides. It took half an hour before Mr. Loring could be bothered to look for his missing employee. "Mel, where the hell are you?" were his last words.

Mr. Loring walked Mel's route, and Orlo was waiting in the darkness again where the only thing that could give him away were the whites of his eyes. For Mr. Loring, he opted for the throat but missed slicing him clean across his jowls. The effect was more or less the same. The devil's eyes gleamed with moisture as his body silently spasmed in the dirt. Orlo hoped hell was hotter than the Southern summer, but he doubted it. Mr. Loring would fit right in.

Patrols were still about, so he had to be fast. He set off a mile north, carefully avoiding anyone of any color that was in his way. Behind a rest stop, his guide was waiting for him, a slender man with quick feet and a map built into his brain. They moved faster than the eye could see; neither one of them had to slow down for the other. They ran toward the docks. There Orlo paid his guide for a small sailboat as well as directions to navigate the North Atlantic to Anda island. He had never sailed before, and he certainly did not have a clue as to how to keep a sense of direction in the vast blue plains. He sailed for several weeks, avoiding starvation and bullying waves (as well as another slave ship) before he shipwrecked on the shores of the African Gulf. The locals of the land were understandably happy that the seas had brought them a black man for once, and they hosted him graciously for a short time before pointing him in the right direction, west of their villages.

It was only by chance that he reached the island on the day of his brother's deputy naming. If it had been any other day, the Kialli locals would have been more likely to notice the arrival of a stranger and might have been confrontational. His previous hosts had gifted him with a canoe to reach Anda. It was well built, but he struggled to keep his dominance over the tiny thing when a storm set in. His canoe was the David to the North Atlantic's Goliath, but the vessel had reigned supreme in the end, even if it was not exactly in one piece. He was home. With the winds still gusting and his breaths still coming out in short bursts, he arched his back, summoned whatever strength remained in him, and hauled the wreckage inland. He then searched for a bag of provisions he had brought along. A handful of milkweed and some papaya slices—his final and only splurges as a slave—went down the hatch. With no steed and all of his provisions downed, he walked further inland for what seemed like forever until after even sorer feet a village came into view. When he saw the village, something was induced in the confines of his cranium. Two pieces of thought long unconnected then touched intimately, and Orlo, the memory, remembered once more.

XI

MALAGASY: Hatrany Am-bohoka
|| ENGLISH: From the Womb

A single unknown visitor interrupted the climax of the celebration. It had been one person's gasp and then another and another until bit by bit the crowd hinted at a stranger's arrival. He had a thick beard, and every piece of clothing he wore was tattered and an off-putting yellow, as if his wardrobe had been ransacked by pointy things and rubbed strenuously with maize. The exposed parts of his body showed hideous scars that told of his torment, although no one knew what sort of ordeal he had been through. Some of the guards were growing worried as the man walked closer to the king, but the king remained calm. By the time the man finally reached the king, the celebration had stopped. Silence in the form of a cough and sound of crickets took hold of the event. No one spoke. No one moved. The king scanned the man in front of him suspiciously. Takloh growled under his breath, annoyed by the pause in a day that was his to play through.

"Who are you?" the king asked.

The man said nothing. He only looked at the king and Takloh in silence.

"Speak!" the king demanded.

Takloh was the first person to realize who the man was. In a fraction of a second, he had lunged at him. At first, everyone thought he had grown tired of the man's refusal to talk and that his anger had gotten the best of him, but Takloh did not strike. Instead, he embraced him. The two of them rolled affectionately on the floor. Takloh was ecstatic. Tears rolled down his cheeks, and his cries were louder than the music had been.

"You know this man?" the king finally asked after they had hugged long enough.

"Baba!" Takloh shouted. "Look at this man. View him well, and tell me you do not know who he is!"

Cries from the crowd came as someone else recognized the man. The man stopped hugging his brother and stood to his feet so the king could have another look at him. The tears were contagious, and the king caught them. They rolled profusely down his cheeks and the mystery man's as well. The people of the committee were not sure what to make of what was going on, but they were interested and so watched.

"People!" the king shouted, trying to get the attention he already had. "The elders have unearthed my suffering even though I thought I had done well to hide it. This man"—the king pointed to him—"he is my long-lost second born. Most of my older subjects know of whom I speak."

There were ohs and ahs as most of the older people remembered the king's kidnapped son.

"Today marks the day of Orlo's return!" the king exclaimed.

Those not old enough to know about Orlo had heard tales of what had taken place on that fateful day. A cheering louder and more thunderous than ever before broke out. The cries were intense; the yelling rose up, as did the sound of music that played right on cue. The night was deafeningly loud, and everyone was happy. The memory would not be forgotten again.

After the celebration, the king invited Orlo into the kraal and asked that all of his children also be present. Khyik had never known his second-eldest brother, so he was intrigued that the man who sat before him, a man who looked older than Takloh and whose severe features beat the king's, was of his own blood. It put a hope in him that one day he might grow to be so manly and rugged. How Orlo had gotten that way was something Khyik did not want to experience. When Orlo asked about his mother, he received the answer that she was dead. No one expected him to cry, and he did not cry. All he did was run his fingers through his overgrown hair and sigh impatiently, as if her being dead was a problem that could be fixed. The king was overjoyed, and he did not want his joy to be dampened by her memory, one that had no chance of coming back, so he urged his son to tell him everything. Orlo was reluctant at first, but he looked around the candlelit room and at all the hands and feet that were not in chains or shackles or cuffs. The faces he saw were ones of free people and furthermore his family, so he told them everything. It took hours for him to tell it all, and it still was not everything. By the time he had finished, it was daybreak. Khyik had been awestruck by his long-lost brother's resilience but heartbroken by his sad tales. Takloh had nodded understandingly, even though in reality it probably took a slave to understand one. The king had looked troubled the whole time. He smiled as Orlo told his story, but he felt immense pain for his son. And although he would not dare say it aloud, he would not have had a second child if he had known what it would have to go through. Nyari was the quietest; she almost did not breathe as she listened, as though she was afraid her lungs might cause her to miss something important. When Orlo had finished talking, the king sent him to take a bath. He also sent servants to fetch him new clothes and dispersed the family meeting.

At midday, after everyone had finished sleeping, the king called for the meeting to resume. This time Orlo was the one asking the questions and soliciting tales. The first thing on his mind was why the king had allowed Europeans to inhabit the island. He had risked so much to come home only to find what he had been running away from. When the king explained the deal that the Kialli had formed with them, Orlo was displeased.

"How can you form deals with those people?" he asked. "In their lands, they torture us and cause us perpetual grief."

Orlo's Kialli was shabby at best, but it surprised everyone how much he remembered. He was not wearing any clothing on his upper body, and the marks of the white man's whip were tattooed on his back and arms. The lines were plentiful and had been heinously inflicted.

"It is for the greater good of the island, for the greater good of our people," the king explained.

"And what of my brother? The one born after me? How do you think he fares in their lands?" Orlo asked.

"I think as long as we have the Cobbleton boy as our ward, he will be fine," the king replied.

Orlo was not satisfied. He would have rather seen the king come to his senses and slaughter every person of other, but they had Anen, who was the boy born after him, the brother he had yet to meet. With everything that had happened in the past day, he had not taken the time simply to admire his family. Takloh was just as he had remembered him, even though he was much, much larger. He was still headstrong and authoritative. He had not remembered his baba very well. Even then, the man looked as unfamiliar as he must have looked to him when he returned. His sister was beautiful; she reminded him of his mother. She looked so much like her that he had thought Nyari to be his mother at first but then quickly corrected himself; his mother would not look *younger* after all the years he had been away. Then there was the youngest child, the one named Khyik. Orlo had mistaken him for a servant or at best the son of a lesser chief and not of his own blood. The boy was unimpressive. He did not provoke fear with his presence, he did not cause people to reminisce about a late queen, and he had not been privy to learning in distant lands; he was just a boy like any other. He would have died on the plantation. His hands were the type to lose blood easily, and his soft skin would have deteriorated quickly under the blow of a whip as it was too dark to merit indoor work. Anen was the only one he had not met. Whenever he did meet Anen, his family would finally be reunited again, every missing piece in its place except for the one who bore most of the lot. Still, Orlo was optimistic that maybe when his family was reunited, he would be able to cast his past away into some stark hell; there his history might meet the devil he slayed.

As the day went on, the family stayed together, catching up on lost time. Orlo found that he could not enjoy his return home when the enemy was always in view. He had not needed to kill Mr. Loring, but if he had not, a part of him would have died.

Every time he saw a pale face with feet on his home, *his* dark soil that matched *his* tinge, something rattled in him. Orlo had developed something over his years of torment. It was something that he could not express openly as a slave but something that he chose to express on the night of his escape. It had grown with him, made root in him, and now it was blossoming foul flowers, the types that killed anything that ate them and irritated anything they came into contact with. Never was a racist autodidactically so, but he was. He had taught himself to hate the white man discreetly. But without shackles to suppress this hatred, it was running carefree. He had a feverish desire to spill blood to satisfy his hatred, and he needed the blood to be white.

The first time this hatred had taken a hold of him had been at the sight of Khyik and Samuel playing in the village square together. It had been high noon, and the normally overexposed sun was covered by some clouds, so the boys had thought it a good idea to play chase with some of the younger children. He had been sitting down on some grass and watching over the children along with Nyari. He was trying to get her to tell him more about Anen when Samuel's laughter triggered something in him. Nyari had noticed his hatred early on, but there was little she could do about it. Who was she to tell a slave that it was wrong for him to hate his master's race? The thing was, Samuel was not his master; like Khyik, he was only a boy. When hatred layered on top of itself over and over again, it achieved properties akin to a psychedelic drug; Orlo's had layered tenfold over this point. Even before he knew what he was doing, Samuel Cobbleton's neck was in his grip. The boy's eyes dilated, and his orangey-gold hair flopped helplessly; he was terrified from head to toe. Orlo had lifted him away from the ground with a single, veiny arm and spiteful fingers. A few village men saw him and rushed to Samuel's aid.

"What has he done?" they asked as they ran to loosen Orlo's grip. "Elders have mercy if you kill the child!" they warned.

Khyik did not know what to do. When the men freed Samuel, Orlo shook his head as if to fix his mind. Then without saying a word, he receded into the kraal.

"What is wrong with him?" Khyik asked angrily.

Samuel was coughing throatily on the ground. The village men lingered for a few moments to make sure Samuel was not dying, and then they too receded back into their tasks.

"He does not like the people of other," Nyari said.

Samuel had ended his coughing and was listening in to find out why he had been assaulted.

"I do not care!" Khyik testified. "He cannot just cause harm whenever he wishes!"

Khyik inspected Samuel, and Samuel held up his hand to show that he was all right.

"I would prefer that didn't happen again," Samuel said, scratching his neck.

"Orlo," Nyari started, "he was a slave. You do not know some of the things he has seen. He has told us many, but I fear there are things that have affected him greatly."

"That does not give him the right to harm my friend!" Khyik shouted.

"Yes, I know," Nyari agreed. "I will try to speak with him, or if he will not listen to me, then I will have Baba or Takloh speak to him. But, Khyik…"

Khyik met his sister's gaze and listened closely.

"It would be wise to keep Samuel away from Orlo, at least for the time being."

Khyik took this advice to heart and did his best to keep Samuel away from his ill-tempered brother. He succeeded most of the time, but even with his cautiousness, he could not avoid the occasional clash. It always caught him off guard. Samuel would look at something for a few moments too long—it did not even have to be Orlo that he was looking at, just as long as he looked at it for a period of time that did not suit Orlo. Orlo would become taken with animosity and need to be restrained from making Samuel's face concave.

His son's lack of restraint did not please the king, but Nyari had been right in her train of thought. It was only natural for a slave to hate the race of his master. Despite whatever right Orlo had for loathing Samuel, the king did his best to deter his son from disturbing the already-fragile peace.

XII

SESOTHO: Le Bothata Ba
ENGLISH: Trouble

He watched from afar, solitary, solemn faced, and knee deep in beige shrubbery. His gaze was set far away on the plains, on a pride of lions, rulers of a wilderness that was technically under his control. The thick mane of a male fluttered up and down like the silky wings of a butterfly. The male was followed closely by five lionesses. All six tails that finished with tawny tufts of fur bobbed into a dark, tree-studded African horizon. With one fearsome roar and a few strides, they were out of sight. Mana knew where they were headed. The Elder River was not far off. In a few strides, the lions would be at its bank, and in a few paddles, they would be out of his domain. So it seemed that the animals were choosing the Kialli side too, just as the men of other had.

"Very well," he thought.

He would not be bothered by it. For him, he needed only the favor of the elders and nothing more. Still it was circulating that the men of other had presented the Kialli with many wonders and gifts, which had led his people to question if the elders really did favor their counterparts on the other side of the river. It did not help that a period of misfortune had plagued the Domka. During the last rainy season, on the Domka side of the island, the rains did not come. Drought had caused most of their plants to fail and ushered in a food shortage. Luckily, only a few people had died, and among them most were children and not useful men. Mana would not admit it, even to himself, but he had begun to doubt the elders too. Even after recovering from an unproductive yesteryear, the Domka had at best a mediocre season. They had not grown in number. Their cattle had actually decreased in number; they had the lions to thank for that. And now it seemed that the Kialli were in a deal so lucrative that even his own people never failed to talk about it. He had made a law against discussing Kialli matters, but if he enforced it every time it was broken, he would not have subjects to rule over. Although the rumors varied, one thing was certain: the safety of the white boy was the pin keeping all of their dealings together. If the elders were not on his side, he would not be on theirs. This thought was one that he would not dare say aloud; even for kings, the punishment was death. But if the Kialli were on the road to being the chosen people, he knew he had to stop them. They were the inferior people, and he would prove this to the elders by ruling over them forcibly. This would not be an easy thing to do. It would require drastic action, something risky and deliberate to discombobulate the other half. The way Mana saw it, he had no choice. A pride might have departed from his domain, but not from him.

It was one day while out on a routine Kialli hunting expedition that Samuel realized, for the first and last time, the true capacity of his heart. He knew he would not be on the island forever, but he also knew that she would remain in his head forever if he did not act. So what used to be relaxed conversation, chatting easily, became nerve-racking conversation without colloquialism. He took the time to choose his words, so when the sentences did finally come out of his mouth, although the texture in his speech may have been jagged, anyone who heard could tell that what he was saying had been crafted and not blurted. Only a few weeks earlier and Samuel would never have done this, but there was something about her that changed him. He had seen it happen to some of the men at port cities who had eyed the inland damsels come to gaze at the sea. The man would step too close to the woman of his interest, and then suddenly his face would glow the natural red rouge of lust and his throat would dry up as if he had just swallowed a thirsty talcum that, in quenching its own hydrophilic thirst, also brought drought to the man's gullet. Vulnerable. That was what he was, and it had nothing to do with the lack of guards keeping watch over him.

Even when the Domka arrow struck him in his side, immediately ending his life, his brain still held an image of the dazzling Nyari, and his heart still throbbed for her if only for a few moments more.

Fate was a cruel thing. It could not be pleaded with, and it had no sympathy for the vulnerable.

Khyik was not far behind Samuel when the arrow struck, and even though he could not see his friend's demise through the thick bush, he knew something was wrong. Just a few seconds after Samuel had been hit, a scout, realizing the danger, blew into an ivory vuvuzela, and the tumultuous drone of it let all of the Kialli know that they were under attack. The Domka assailants, having lost any element of surprise, then broke out into war cries.

"Ahhhh-ye-ye-ye-ye-ye-ye!" they called out.

The Kialli men were quick to ready themselves. Any man holding a scythe had a firm grip on it with the sharp end pointed toward suspect parts of the green surrounding. Any man with a blow dart had his lungs ready. Any man with a bow had it drawn with the arrow twitching anxiously for a victim.

"Ahhhh-ye-ye-ye-ye-ye-ye!"

The first wave of Domka attackers emerged from the bush. As sounds of scythes, screams, and parting flesh filled the forest, what had once been an orderly hunting party was now a scrambled mess of men and murder. Not knowing who was who or what was what, Khyik took to the only place he thought safe: the trees. He found a young afrormosia and darted up its hull. As he did so, his left ear picked up the sound of an arrow missing his head. Flecks of bark from the tree dug into his uncallused hands, but he did not dare stop. He winced through the pain as he tried to block out the screams. The men below him screamed like a lamb screamed while it was being held down and slaughtered. They screamed desperately, and only after the life was escaping them did their screams die down to throaty, terminal croaks. When Khyik did stop climbing, he was some thirteen meters or so above the forest floor; from there he could see everything. He could see combatants still swinging, still firing, still hunting each other down through the viridescent vegetation. He could see bodies, almost all of them with their eyes wide open and staring back at him.

He was about to cry when he saw a body in the clearing. Through a hole in the canopy, a beam of sunlight irradiated the dead boy; he saw what were the remains of an angelic casualty, one whose skin was quaintly imbued with the powder frost of faultlessness. The boy had his eyes closed, and were it not for the pool of blood he lay in and the arrow butt peeking out of his chest, he would have looked peaceful. He looked as though he had been thinking of something sweet when he died, and it was this thought that kept Khyik from crying. Slowly he descended from the tree. There were still sounds of fighting not too far away from him, but he did not care. When he reached the bottom, he wiped away flecks of bark still implanted in his hands and walked over to Samuel's body. He stooped down and looked hard at his friend. Then he reached out his hand, not to alter his friend in any way—the scene of Samuel's death had been quite picturesque—but to grab a handful of orange flowers that were on the ground. Khyik put the flowers in his mouth and munched away at them until he could feel bitter liquid trickling down his throat. The flowers he had consumed were known tonics, drugs known to speed the heart and heighten the senses.

He grabbed a stray Domka spear as the tonic started to take effect. Everything he saw had a red tinge to it, and he began foaming a little at the mouth. He recalled everything he had ever learned about fighting, and taking one last look at his friend, he darted off into the greenery, angry and ready for war.

XIII

ZULU: Isikhathi Sempi ||
ENGLISH: A Time for War

What had once been a serene landscape was now stretched out and wrung so thoroughly that any remnants of tranquility had vanished. Copper African dirt seemed bolder but not quite as brilliant; perhaps it was responsible for the bloodshot sky. Trees that had once been tall were now cut short into dead horizontal rows. Land once young had gone through a sort of demonic puberty; it appeared the island was now the chosen spot for hell on earth. That was what it had become: an anti-Eden, a war zone, but somehow still home. Khyik tried to remember which omnipresent elder had believed that chaos was the natural order of things and that real order was in fact a dangerous construct of man. He ran through the list of names in his head to keep himself from thinking too much about what he was seeing. The name never came.

What he saw was reminiscent of the night when he had seen the dead man in the kraal's compound, only now he had daylight to make the dead and dying even harder to look away from. This only became worse once he came out of the forest. The desolation was incomprehensible. Thatched roofs that had once stood on top of humble huts were brought down to a kneel, and the huts' walls had been uprooted, like poppy weeds in cropland by farmers, so that only the private contents of unsheltered homes remained. Khyik saw an overturned table and pieces of what had once been clay pots in the naked hut. The owners of the items were a few feet away, still and on their stomachs. A hen strolled ignorantly past them until the sound of men grunting caused it to spook and flee in clumsy flight. One man pushed the other, so the less fortunate of the two tripped over a corpse. The man who was standing picked up a scythe from the ground. The man on the floor scrambled to get to his feet, but the man with the scythe kicked him in the throat and ended any hope of a fair fight. The man with the scythe was a Domka, and it was then that Khyik noticed how hard he was gripping his spear. The Domka man stepped over the corpse and closer to the Kialli man, who held his neck and spat out blood.

"We will tear your kind apart," the Domka man said. "We will rip away whatever crown you thought was fused to your skull." The man raised up his scythe in preparation. "We will erase your likeness so that you may only exist under Domka rule."

Khyik raised up his spear so that it was at the same height as his head. He took one step back and aimed so that the tip of the spear was roughly on the path of the Domka man's head. The scythe went down as Khyik let go. Possibly from the excitement of war, Khyik found that he had more brawn. The spear left his hand in an instant and sped through the air silently until it came into contact with its target. The scythe hit the ground. The spear had entered the Domka soldier in the abdomen and not in the head. The Domka man did not scream; he only looked down and trembled at the sight. He was impaled. The spear had entered his side from the left, and the tip of the spear poked out of him at his right. He stumbled a few times and then fell to his knees. The Kialli man got up, and Khyik recognized him as one of the farmers from the village. The farmer did not thank Khyik; he only nodded, picked up the scythe, and ran toward the sound of fighting somewhere else. Khyik inched toward the wounded man, taking larger and larger steps as he gained more courage. When he got to the man, he had to keep from recoiling from the sight of so much blood. His feet were soaked in it. The wounded man was still breathing, and he looked at Khyik. He did not look at Khyik accusingly, only to look at him as if to say, "Ah, so this is my killer. There he is."

Khyik grabbed the end of the spear. The wounded man let out weak moans but did not break eye contact. Khyik gritted his teeth and pulled his weapon out from the man. He heard the slush of organs as it exited the man's body. Now his spear was red and lubricated. Blood leaked out, covering more ground like high tide on a bank until the wounded man let out his last breath and died. Getting as good a grip on his slimy spear as he could manage, Khyik darted off in the direction the farmer had gone. He was amazed at how his surroundings had changed to accommodate the heinous events that were taking place. The very air he breathed had gone from smelling like dew to smelling like death. Screams replaced chirping birds, and destruction was as widespread as civilization. He jogged among all of it, embracing it and calling on a power much greater than himself. But it seemed the faster Khyik jogged, the further away the screams became and the more dead bodies he saw. He was going to turn a corner and continue his scouting when he heard someone call out his name.

It was Nyari. She had caught sight of him from behind a partially standing hut. Khyik was overjoyed, but he stopped himself from screaming. He dropped his spear, ran over to her, and hugged her, trying his best not to get blood on her.

"Oh, Khyik!" Nyari cried. Tears poured down her face like waterfalls, and Khyik held her so close to himself that it almost hurt. "They are killing everyone."

"It is all right, my sister," Khyik comforted. "I will protect you."

But Nyari kept sobbing. "You do not understand. The men who refuse to surrender have their eyes gouged before they are killed. The women...the Domka take them as wives and violate them, and any child who remains loyal is..."

Nyari could not finish, as her sobbing got the best of her. She cried like a child, so he hugged her like a parent.

"You must leave this place," he said.

Nyari stopped crying. She backed away from him and frowned with a pained expression that made Khyik feel guilty for saying it. But there was no other choice.

"Nyari, you must leave. Mana will have you for his wife," Khyik said.

"I would die before I would marry him!" she barked.

"I know. That is why you must leave," Khyik held.

Nyari looked stunned, and then, all at once, her face was sorrowful. She hugged Khyik again.

"Where will I go?" she asked, her question muffled by Khyik's chest.

"Go to the edge of the island. There are always boats there. You know how to row, so it should not be too difficult. You must go to the mainland," Khyik instructed.

"What if I get lost?" she asked.

She broke away from him and looked at him. Khyik started to remember his mother again, but he cut off the memory. He had to remain focused.

"There is an island that Takloh showed me," he said.

He cradled her in his arms while giving her the instructions to get there. "Do you understand? After you have continued on for a few minutes, go just left, okay?"

Nyari nodded.

"Go there, and after you have rested, head to the mainland. Samuel has died, and the men of other will punish us no doubt. If the Kialli have control of the island after this, there will not be enough of us to fight them off, and if the Domka have control, they will be no match for them. Either way, there will only be more death. Go," he said, gently pushing her away.

Nyari hesitated for a moment. She reached out to him but only touched air. Her brother was right in front of her, but already he felt so far away. She turned around, still sniffling, and then disappeared into the trees.

He watched her leave, watched her get swallowed up by Mother Nature, knowing that he would most likely never see her again.

For a period, there was a complete halt in space and time. Everything stood still. Khyik's mind did not center on one thing but wrapped its reach around the entirety of the inconceivable, the conflict that persisted to no end except to the end of both sides. It was a cyclical conflict, one that resembled a snake devouring itself endlessly, never appeased and never allowed to die. He saw all the damage and ruin that went beyond that which was tangible; he saw the torment of what was not.

His epiphany was badly timed. A hard object knocked him upside the head. He fell on his back and looked up, dazed and confused. Domka men had circled him, and one of them had snuck up on him and hit him with something. Khyik was not shocked until he noticed what the man had hit him with. It was a severed head without eyes; the man gripped it by the hair. Its facial features drooped and were swollen, and its tongue was sticking out. Khyik covered his mouth with his hand to stop himself from vomiting. He could see the brain in one of the eye sockets and the cord where the eyeball had been connected in another. It was Orlo. He had lost a brother, gained him back, and then lost him again. So it went.

He found himself war-ready again and eyed his spear. It was lying on the ground just a few feet away from him, but the man who held the head caught on. Before Khyik could make a move, the man advanced. He pulled out a small blade and stabbed Khyik in the back. Then he struck Khyik with the severed head again, hard. Everything went black.

When Khyik woke up, he found himself walking, and he knew he was walking to the end. He raised his head and squinted at the too-bright sky. They had come to a clearing, and the Domka soldiers formed a circle around him. He looked left and right, trying to figure out why they had stopped.

"Let me see the boy," a voice boomed from behind him.

Khyik turned around to face Mana himself. The man was as large as men came, and his voice was deeper than the deepest parts of the Elder River. Mana did not look at all tired, which made sense because his attack on the Kialli had been swift and nearly effortless.

"Ah, and here is the boy of the dead king," Mana boomed.

The Domka soldiers laughed at his remark.

"I am the king now, and I advise you to execute me quickly," Khyik retorted.

He did not know why he said that, but he was glad that he had. It could be true for all he knew. First his brother Orlo had been thought to be dead, then *not* Orlo when it was discovered he was alive. Then it was his brother Anen, who was surely to be killed by the Europeans now that the peace had been broken, then his brother Orlo again when he had actually been killed, and now it was likely Takloh and his baba, which left only him alive.

"Young man, why are you so eager to die? There is still life to be lived, and you do not have to suffer the same fate as your baba or the rest of his kin. I will allow you to live under my rule as my servant." Mana's face was now close enough for Khyik to smell the wine that the Domka must have stolen from the king's quarters.

"You drink the wine gifted by the men who sought to destroy our people?" Khyik asked.

"You are the ones who accepted the wine," Mana pointed out.

"Out of diplomacy," Khyik countered.

"Never mind it. It is fitting. This wine belongs to men who sought to destroy your people, and it seems that today we are those men." Mana smiled as the Domka soldiers raised their weapons in agreement and cheered.

"We are the same people!" Khyik shouted, hot with anger. "Were we not one kin long ago, and if that is true, are we not one kin now?"

Mana took a step back, drew back his hand, and slapped Khyik hard so that the sound echoed in the chaos. A drop of blood rolled down Khyik's cheek from where Mana's nail had dug into him with the slap.

"No," Mana whispered as he took a swig of the drink, "we are not. Do not try to play the hand of a man above war. Do not lie to yourself. The Kialli would have done the same thing my people are doing now, only quicker, if they had the white man's guns. Even now the white men here are shooting Kialli and Domka indiscriminately. Without the boy, there is no pact, and when the men of other send for reinforcements to avenge him, I would rather see them take us both down."

He puckered his lips as he thought about what to do with Khyik. When he had thought long and hard and arrived at an idea, he turned to one of his subjects.

"Send for Mikemba," he ordered.

The Domka man ran away for a few minutes and then returned with someone. He was a boy similar in age to Khyik; they were similar in height too. In fact, the only real difference between them was how their faces looked. The boy Mana called Mikemba looked a lot like Mana himself. Khyik could see that Mikemba was Mana's son. Mana motioned for Mikemba to come closer, and the boy obeyed. Once the two men, baba and son, were standing side by side, Mana whistled for a knife to be brought to them and then handed it to Mikemba.

He gave his son two hard pats on the back. "Kill him," he ordered.

Mikemba walked up to Khyik until they were face-to-face. When Khyik looked into Mikemba's eyes, he saw his own reflection, and when Mikemba looked into Khyik's eyes, he saw his own reflection. The two boys were standing so close that their afros touched; spindly rogue hairs made contact with one another.

On the most horrendous of days stood two boys; one of them had been born on one side of an island and the other boy on the other side. Now they observed one another, taking in every difference they could find between themselves but finding that there were not that many. In a different time, they might have been able to respect one another, to have a mutual understanding, to coexist with love, but this was a time for war. In the blink of an eye, Mikemba's knife was lodged deep in Khyik's chest. Khyik fell backward to chants of "Hoorah!" from the onlookers. From his mouth, a steady stream of red escaped and watered the dry dirt. The knife glistened in light, and his eyes closed forever.

The three of them laughed. They spent a long time just enjoying the sight—the sheet of silver cast on the surface of the water by the moon, the white sand, the clear black sky dotted with white diamonds…it was all so beautiful.

An executive order from the right spirit could mean one grave too few, and the Reaper would protest but be powerless to intervene.

"Was that all Pete was worth? Nothing more than the nickels and dimes,"

His feet were the color of burnished bronze, refined in a furnace, and his voice was like a waterfall.

Part II

The Present

XIV

W itt sat back on his sofa and eyed the clock. The second hand was taking too long again, and he considered seriously that it could be broken. It wouldn't be the first time he'd bought a bad clock. The one hung up on the wall had been the third just that month alone... or was it the fourth? Not that it mattered. Witt could go through eighteen clocks if need be; he just didn't understand what was so damn hard about making a clock that actually worked. He licked his fingers and brushed the last few specs of white powder off the corner of his mahogany coffee table. Witt smiled with satisfaction.

It had taken the help most of the morning to clean up the aftermath of last night's party. While his house was being cleaned, he was out shopping, although these days it was hard to find things that he didn't already own. He ended up settling for another leather jacket. It was barely fall, but he liked the way it looked, the way it draped over him and made every step that he took look necessary, as if he planned the way his legs moved. He hadn't even wanted it at first, but he saw the way the employee at the men's clothing store had looked at him, the way that older gentleman assumed that he couldn't afford it, the way he had tried to gesture, rather condescendingly, to the cheaper aisles. That was what had made Witt *need* it. That happened often, and when it did, it was bittersweet. First came a wave of anger and resentment because of their assumptions, but then he would find a price tag with a few more digits, coolly pull out his credit card, and swipe confidently. Store after store, item after item, waiting for the cashier's eyebrows to rise in surprise. He lived for that turning point, when people realized how much money he really had and became embarrassed or, better yet, ashamed of themselves.

But after he made the purchase, the euphoria left him. He'd wear it or use it, whatever it was, once, maybe twice, and then it was as good as gone, fading to irrelevance. That same jacket was hung on the coatrack along with all the others. At one point, the coatrack was almost dislodged from the wall because of all the weight. He didn't see his greed as a fault. No, that would imply that something was wrong with him. He viewed it as a personality trait, a trait of the powerful. He often thought that was the reason most of his friends had left. They were weak, and his presence had made them subordinate. That must've been the reason. It wasn't his fault that he had made it and they hadn't. Still, all the money in the world couldn't erase his memories of growing up with them. Thankfully, falling out with his friends hadn't been particularly painful. Whether it was Gordon, Wesley, or Duke, the story was always the same. They were jealous, each with his own case of the green-eyed monster. They wanted what only he could achieve, so one by one, they left.

At first, he'd been devastated, but over time, he'd come to accept their betrayals as what could only be described as petty acts of envy. He was the god that they refused to believe in.

Witt shifted his gaze on to a half-emptied pack of cigarettes on the coffee table; each elongated cylinder of momentary relief beckoned to him. He pulled one out from the box and produced a lighter from his back pocket. He lit the cigarette before tossing the lighter onto the table. He lodged the cigarette between his lips and inhaled deeply. The clock on the wall still ticked. The second hand's every movement echoed through the halls as smoke danced up from his mouth to the chandelier. He looked up and admired it, a crown sparkling above his head that declared him the sole escapee of the proletariat. He loved to revel in his success.

But sometimes he wished he could go back, if not for a week or a day, then for just a moment. Usually he tried with every ounce of mental strength to dispel these thoughts. If you were not prepared to drastically change, either for better or worse, then being rich was not for you. And, boy, oh boy, had he changed. In the calm cool dark of his living room, he let his mind wander back to the old days filled with cold water and dark rooms neglected by electricity. Witt's brain tried its best to recreate the noises of the children who played in the street outside his house. That street now served as an entrance to a condominium, but back then, it was sacred ground for those too young to join gangs and too old to die young.

On Saturday mornings, laughter rang out instead of gunshots. A pair of bodies dashed across the street, one after the other, both alive, a harmless game of cat and mouse. For Witt, tag was too tame; he liked to play basketball in the street with the older boys. Jermaine carried out the games and functioned as both referee and star player, Riley led group stretches, and James made sure the ball was aired up enough to bounce. Instead of having the basketball hoops adjacent to the sidewalk, Jermaine had thought it better to have both hoops parallel to the sidewalk right smack in the middle of the road. This put them directly in front of oncoming cars. The idea was that when a car was spotted, everyone would have to stop playing and hurry to lift both hoops out of the way until it passed. Although cumbersome, it meant that everyone had to stay alert and learn to work together—at least this was a side effect (really the streets were narrow enough and the houses close enough together that no one wanted to have to deal with a mistimed pass breaking somebody's window). Even so sometimes nobody noticed a vehicle, and the cussing and honking that ensued could turn even the friendliest Saturday b-ball game into a boxing match.

One day, Jermaine suggested having a dedicated lookout. Most of the boys wanted to focus on the game—after all, how else would they achieve broadcast-worthy ball skills? But Pete, Witt's best friend, wasn't as anxious to play, so when the time came to pick a lookout, Pete was the only one who volunteered.

He was good at his job; a car never had to stop and honk while he was on watch. He didn't find his job difficult, though it did take effort to break his eyes away from his comic books, which were a distraction, yet they miraculously never got in the way of his watchkeeping. Witt joined Pete from time to time when he wasn't a part of an ongoing game. And on rare occasions, Pete would proceed to share his comic book, and they would read it together. Pete could only afford the cheapest comics; most of his were secondhand copies. This love of comic books stayed with Pete well into adulthood, and Witt routinely helped feed the addiction. There wasn't any logical reason for the financial backing of Pete's impulsive comic book buying as an adult other than it was an excuse to spend time with someone who was now looking to be his only friend. Witt even bought Pete a gold chain, made to look like one of Pete's favorite comic book characters, Dark Eon. It was nothing more than nickels and dimes to him. Pete, on the other hand, had been ecstatic since the chain was ludicrously expensive, well made, and Witt was normally stingy with gifts. To Pete, it was worth so much more than money, and Witt couldn't suppress his joy at his own kindness, especially since Pete wore it religiously from the moment he'd received it.

Witt's cigarette lost its kick, and the last flakes of ash descended to the carpet. He pulled himself out of his thoughts and got up from the couch. Pete was now forty-five minutes late. Witt had called multiple times only to be answered by an all-too-familiar raspy voice mail. He was in the middle of dialing again when something caught his attention; just behind his curtain, a dash of light illuminated bits of fall leaves suspended in the air. He recognized the headlights of Pete's car.

Witt walked up to the curtain and pulled it aside to reveal the scene. His cigarette dropped from his mouth. He didn't stop to pick it up. He didn't grab his expensive leather jacket on his way out of the door of his extravagant house. He didn't feel the numbing cold pinching his skin as the breeze hit him. He didn't feel anything at all. In fine black wool socks, he walked across his lawn, his feet crushing every auburn leaf set in rigor mortis along the way. Three neatly stacked bullet holes decorated the half-open driver-side window. The whites of Pete's eyes were showing, his chapped lips gave no air, his body emitted no warmth, and his body harbored no life. The only thing the corpse was missing was a gold necklace.

As Witt shakily lifted his phone to call the police, he thought to himself, "Was that all Pete was worth? Nothing more than the nickels and dimes to some fool with a gun and a hankering for a comically costly gold chain?"

Without a doubt, a gang had done this; to them, they only saw dangling money. Never mind that Pete would choose a set of eight comics over an eight-ball ten out of ten times. That hadn't mattered none. A single man couldn't shoot someone from multiple angles at one time. A pack had pierced its prey and in doing so pierced themselves with many pangs.

The police arrived in no time at all but not because it was a murder. In a quiet little cubby of black poverty not too far away from his neighborhood, nine people had just been shot; there was more murder over there. Simple math would tell you that nine was greater than one, but a simple cop would tell you that that wasn't true if the *one* happened to live in Palmstock Court. Witt hit the little X icon next to the notification at the top of his phone screen, and the little rectangle that said "In Your Area: Nine Shot Dead" disappeared.

Pete's body was strapped onto a gurney and loaded onto an ambulance like cargo; there was no saving him. Witt wished he had chosen to accept the blanket offered to him. He felt a thousand degrees colder than whatever the forecast had said—frozen whole and to the bone. Men in long coats with clipboards in their hands huddled around the bullet-riddled Lincoln. The siren lights bathed the car in blue and red, and for just a moment, it looked like something a superhero might drive. A policeman with square shoulders, hairy arms, and eyes that said "Better Palmstock than the projects" asked him a few more questions. There was nothing he couldn't answer.

"How long have you known Mr. Burgan?"

"As long as I can remember."

"Do you have any idea who could've done this? Anyone in particular?"

"No, I don't know anyone. No one who knew him could do something like this."

"Did he say anything to you before this happened? Anything that might lead us to his killer?"

"No, Officer."

"Has he mentioned any names in the last few days or weeks? Anyone you haven't heard of before?"

"No, Officer."

"Any strange locations?"

"No, Officer."

"Naturally we'd like to get in touch with Mr. Burgan's family as soon as possible. Do you have his family's contact information?"

"Yes, Officer."

Witt hadn't even thought about how the death of his best friend would affect everyone else. He pulled his phone back out and read the number aloud.

"And who is this person in relation to the victim?"

"One of his younger brothers, Officer."

XV

An executive order from the right spirit could mean one grave too few, and the Reaper would protest but be powerless to intervene. A firm hand shook me awake from some dark place I had no business leaving. Two cat eyes looked me up and down. In return, I studied the brown that pooled in them. When he was done, he got up and walked to the other side of the strangest room I had ever seen. That was when I noticed everything new. My hammock was not a hammock; it was a soft square block with cloth as thin as a fingernail covering it. The hut I was in was made of stones cut cleaner than anything I had ever seen in our village. There was no scent of earth or animal, and I wondered, briefly, if I had lost my sense of smell.

The two young men in the room spoke to each other in a strange language I was surprised to find I knew. I had to make an effort to see them with the lights at the top of our hut shining so bright. That was new too. There were no holes in the roof that would allow for light, but there was still light in the room. Everywhere I looked I found alien things.

"I must be with my ancestors. This strange place must be where they rest," I thought. The man with the cat eyes walked back to me.

"Do you know who I am?" he asked.

"Josiah," I answered before I could shake my head no.

He smiled. "So you ain't half as crazy as the doctor said you might be."

I had no idea how I had known who he was, but I could not deny the fact that I did *know*. The young man was my brother. His name was Josiah, and he had our mother's eyes. For my seventh birthday, he had gotten me building blocks after he found a coupon for the toy store. He was a troublemaker. He had a big bushy afro that took up more and more volume with each passing year. His hair was the color of peanut butter, and it glowed like honey whenever it was in direct sunlight. I knew what peanut butter was. I knew the taste of it. It came from the supermarket, the same place where Mamma would buy the peppers for the stew she made on special occasions. I knew him, but I did not know anything about me. Where was I? Who was I?

"I can't believe Mamma would be so careless and yell out that awful news while you was in the street. I should give her a piece of my mind," Josiah said.

"I'm pretty sure you gave her your whole mind already the way you went off," said the other man.

He was wearing an expensive-looking red leather jacket, and his arms were folded across his chest. A jet-black beard stood out definitively against his caramel complexion, and his close-shave haircut looked as if it hadn't been done more than forty-five seconds ago, it was that fresh. His heavyset eyebrows were scrunched together, so he looked as though he was in perpetual thought. When he caught me looking at him, his brows parted and the edges of his mouth made a slight frown.

"I'm sorry, Cedric" was all he said.

Josiah sat at the edge of my bed and groaned.

"You ain't the one that need to be sorry," he said. "The ones that need to be sorry are the niggas that done this in the first place," he said, a little angrier. "And you can bet who gonna make 'em sorry," he finished, rising from my side.

He took heavy steps on his way out, but not before the man with the jacket blocked his path.

"Don't go and do something stupid now. After everything that's happened, you really want to go out looking for trouble?"

"Get out of my way. You don't know how it works."

"Don't pull that, Jo. We both know I grew up in the same situation you grew up in."

"But you got out, man. Get out my way."

"You really want to get locked up?"

"You ain't my dad. Get out my way."

"And where is your dad? He's not here. Your mother isn't here either. Cedric would've been here all alone if it weren't for us two, and now you want to fool around and take yourself out the picture too, is that it?"

"You ain't smarter than me," Jo said hotly. "Just 'cause you got out and live around them white folk and talk all proper, that don't make you smarter than me."

"I know, I know—"

"No, you don't! You don't understand that them same people who shot Pete is probably right under our nose, probably a few houses down too. It's snakes around us."

There was a knock at the door. The door opened just enough for a shy-looking young nurse to squeeze her head through.

"Is everything okay in here?" she squeaked.

The man with the jacket gave her a big toothy white smile.

"Yes, miss. We were just having a little discussion."

Josiah gave the nurse a look to make her jump out of her uniform. He was about to get his point across, and I didn't think he liked being interrupted. She shrank into herself a little, but another smile from the other man assured her that she wasn't to blame for Jo's evil eye. She smiled weakly, first at the man with the jacket and then at me, before her head backed out of the room the same way it came in. The door closed.

Josiah sighed. "If you live around snakes, you gonna end up growing fangs too."

There was silence for a moment. Then the man with the jacket walked over to me and sat in the place Jo had been sitting. He smiled at me.

"Put the fangs away then."

"What?" Josiah asked.

The man with the jacket patted me on the head. "Put them away. Tonight you two can sleep at my house."

And just like that, having barely been acquainted with where I was at the moment, I was offered someplace new.

At first, I had thought this whole world I was in, this whole body, was some sort of test from the elders, but as time went on, the possibility of it went down. I had taken the form of the one they called Cedric. It was surreal. It was like quickly flipping through someone's diary so that you knew more of what they knew with each page, and by the time you'd reached the end, you might as well have written it yourself. Initially, my head hurt because it felt as though there were two brains occupying the space meant only for one. But everything quickly melded together, his memories and mine, so that this reality was every bit as real to me as the one on the island back when I was alive.

I learned a lot in the arguments that followed in the car ride to the man with the jacket's home (whose name was Witt). Jo and I had apparently lost our older brother, Peter, in a shooting of some kind, and Witt was a close friend of the family and our older brother's best friend. The people who were supposedly my parents were nothing like what my actual parents had been. Back on the island, my father had been a masculine man. A king among men, he always did whatever was in his will to do. His mind knew only how to lead, and his body was cruel and built for either domination or decimation. His body was cocooned with muscles that had been painstakingly earned. The only trouble that seeped through the cocoon was the absence of his late wife.

My new father was troubled by the presence of his current one. He, on the other hand, was a scraggly man. His dominion was over a conveyor belt, which would have been fine if he were at least the king of it. Witt had brought up how our family couldn't put me through school and how it didn't help that our father constantly came home enraged and intoxicated after his boss had given him the (practically) daily threat of unemployment. Up until Witt mentioned this, Jo hadn't been particularly accepting of the idea of living away from the "snakes" that he hated so much, and Witt bringing up our father didn't help things either, no matter how right he was.

"*I'm* gon' put Cedric through school when the time comes," Jo said unconvincingly.

It would have sounded better if he had been trying to convince Witt and not himself.

Witt's eyes watched Jo through a rearview mirror. The indirectness watered down the look, but it was still enough to make Jo look away. Jo had decided to sit in the back with me in case I needed anything. The interior of Witt's car looked as if it had been handcrafted by a team of experts. It was like the shoemaker's elves had transferred into the automotive industry. The leather was so rich that if you touched it and focused hard enough, you could hear the heartbeat of the animal it came from. Wherever plastic would've been found on a lesser car, there was only stainless steel. In every nook you looked in expecting to find faults, you only found more displays of craftsmanship. The floor mats were red velvet, the metal on the seatbelts was real silver, and when I peeked over the driver's seat, I saw that Witt's foot was resting on a gas pedal dipped in red-tinted gold. It was all entirely too much, and it fit him well.

Our mother was a small woman timid to all things except what she claimed as her own; largely, that was us. She lacked the dead queen's grace but surpassed her in kindness. She found comfort in her three musketeers no matter the high jinks we got into. She had made an effort to get Pete all the best comic books when he was younger, even though she found no value in them herself. She was the one who left work to pick up Jo whenever he got suspended; she'd buy him Lorna Doones before she whooped him. She was the one who had pushed me out into our family's hard-knock life. She lit candles when we couldn't pay the lights and read to us when we couldn't keep up with the cable payments. One could only imagine how a mother must have felt when someone she claimed as her livelihood was taken from her.

"They shot my boy! My precious baby boy!"

Some might have said that a morgue was nothing more than a nursery for grown, expired men. For a mother, every child's death was the death of a baby.

I had been in the street doing Lord knows what when I heard her windswept wails, and I froze up like ice. It was an unamused car that made me thaw.

"I haunked, I focking haunked, and ya just stood dair! Dair's a sign that says to keep outta the street. I oughta press charges on ya! Denting up my cah like that. Going all deer-in-the-headlights on me. Do ya know what insurance is, kid?"

We had all agreed to go our separate ways after the accident. My mother was hysterical, of course, having almost lost two of her three children within the span of a few hours. But to the stranger's credit, he did, in fact, honk.

The gates of Palmstock Court housed something precious. An endless row of smooth metallic bars stood upright, tall and proud, corralling the very money that had helped build them. They were like indentured servants, and from the looks of the nice roofs, I could see their masters lived in paradise. In a small boxy booth planted just beside the gates, a worker recognized Witt's car and pressed a button. There was no raspy creek of complaint; the gates opened silently.

These were no huts. Each house took up enough land to support at least forty or fifty huts, maybe more. Thick white columns stood like security guards in front of each brick structure. Every home had a fountain that spouted water clear as the blue island sky. Every home had window panes from top to bottom. Could each of those actually belong to a room? I highly doubted anyone had use for fourteen bedrooms. Back on the island, there would never be that many windows in a hut because as soon as a big storm hit in the rainy season, those windows were as good as holes in a canoe. I doubted these people would have that problem though. They didn't rely on mopane leaves to keep the water out, and even if they did, with houses like these, they could probably afford to pay off the weather.

Eventually, we pulled up to a gray brick mansion. Another large fountain—this one was a sculpture of a naked lady. Her nose hovered over the buds of a rose, and from the center of the flower, water shot out, draping over her before falling back into the depths below to be recirculated. The mansion's little brother was a three-car garage identical in style. I wondered what kind of luxury hid behind the barn-like doors. It would remain a mystery. Witt opted to leave his car in the driveway. He didn't have to turn a key; all he did was get out and the car knew its services were no longer required. For a moment, I thought that the car might be alive, like the livestock we had back on the island. But the last time I checked, animals couldn't stop their hearts on the command, and that was exactly what the car's engine sounded like, the beating heart of a mechanical beast. I think I had expected Witt's house to be somehow smaller than the rest, kind of like how the men of other's ships had been bigger than any of the boats we had on the island. Jo's neck was tilted back so far he stumbled backward and almost fell.

"I knew you had it good, but, damn, you *really* been living it up out here," Jo said.

Witt's cheeks had a faint red tinge to them then, and he smiled. "Ah, c'mon, man, you knew I had this crib," he replied.

"Yeah, yeah, but I ain't never seen it. Goddamn, I still ain't seen the whole thing, and I've been staring at it for a minute now—there's just that much to see."

"Well, come on in. No sense in freezing out here. I'll show you your rooms."

Witt walked right up to his door and opened it.

"He don't even keep his shit locked," Jo whispered to me, chuckling.

"Would you like a tour?" he asked when we got inside.

Sensors picked us up, and a pool of light poured into the foyer.

I would have loved one; it seemed every second brought the promise of seeing something new. A dull pain in my head kept me from saying yes. I held my forehead to keep my brain from breaking through.

Witt saw it and quickly disappeared in a hallway. The foyer was vast. It was at least as big as mine and Jo's house, and although the kraal wasn't small, it was definitely outclassed. A grand staircase with two wooden arms running along the sides of the foyer ended at our feet. Jo gave me two taps on the shoulder. He was looking up at something, so I looked up too. I guess all the light had to have come from somewhere. I remembered that what I was looking at was called a firework. It was circular and had hundreds of little beams of light going outward. But I didn't smell smoke, and this one stayed still.

"That chandelier cost more than life," Jo said.

Witt reemerged from the hallway with a glass of water in one hand and some pills in the other.

"Take this," he ordered.

I downed the pills.

"C'mon, you two, it's late. I'll show you to your rooms for the night."

Witt started up the left wooden arm, and Jo followed behind, grinning ear to ear. It wasn't what I was used to; everything was so foreign and unreal, but I felt calm knowing that even in this realm, I was not without brothers.

XVI

"You'll get him next time," said Xavier.

I wasn't hearing any of it. I wanted to ask if he could get me a Band-Aid, but I didn't want to look weak. My knee was busted up from the fight. As usual I had lost, only this time it was worse.

"Did they really have to record all that though?" I whined.

"They ain't gonna upload it. Feds have already got eyes on him, especially after he pulled that knife on that poor kid. He's an idiot, but even he won't risk letting people put that fight up on Worldstar," he reasoned. "He really got you good," he said, looking me over.

I still tasted blood in my mouth and iron from my swollen lip. Xavier was good at breaking up fights; he had effective muscles that armored his skinny body. It had been Xavier who stopped the fight while everyone else recorded.

"You don't need to go to no hospital now?" he asked.

My bloody knee was starting to soak into the fabric of my jeans, but I shook my head no; I would be all right. Sure, I had gotten the wind knocked out me a couple of times, and I wasn't short on cuts and bruises, but I would be fine.

"Aight then, I got to get home, and if I were you, I would head home too," he advised.

We exchanged a quick fist bump and parted ways. It was a cool Saturday evening in Widower's Grove. It was no Palmstock Court, but in the few weeks I had been living my new life as Cedric, I had accepted it as my new homeland—there were worse places still. I made my way down a menagerie of streets through which only a Widower's Grove local would know how to maneuver until I got to my house. It was dark, but the lights were still on; I knew that wasn't good. If my parents saw me postfight again, I would be in for a lifetime of trouble.

"And here we have the biggest dumbass in Widower's Grove," a voice announced as I walked in.

Jo was in the middle of the living room, sitting on the armrest of the couch. His back was flat against it. His eyes followed me as I walked in.

"All right, all right, just keep your voice down. No need to wake up Mamma and Pops with all that racket," I said.

"How many times do I gotta tell you to stop fighting with that kid? He's gonna seriously mess you up one of these days, and Xavier won't be there to stop it, and I won't be there either to go scare that punk."

Josiah got up to inspect my wounds more closely.

"I'm good, really. He just got a couple of cheap shots in the beginning, that's all," I assured.

There was commotion upstairs.

"Is that Cedric?" Mamma called.

"Go the bathroom. There's a rag in the cupboard. Clean yourself up. Then go put your clothes in the washer and put on a hoodie. If she asks you anything, just keep your head down and say you're cold," Jo instructed.

I nodded and headed for the bathroom.

"Oh, and Cedric," Jo started, "if you get in another fight, make sure your ass wins."

Something in the way he spoke reminded me of Takloh. I smiled, nodded, and went to go clean myself up.

You might have been surprised how easy it was to become acclimated to the life of a completely different person. The transition wasn't as abrasive as you might expect. Widower's Grove was an island in its own way, isolated from the rest of the world, less bucolic but every bit as wild.

I came to know that Cedric Burgan had three good friends: Xavier Jackson, Percy White, and Old Boy. Old Boy's real name was Oliver Beckon, but everyone called him Old Boy because he walked with an aged and somewhat lopsided gait—also because he had what we called "a reverse babyface." His face was chiseled in an ancient way. People always thought Old Boy was the oldest when he was actually the youngest out of all of us.

The oldest member of our crew was Xavier. He was eighteen, and he made it seem as though eighteen was the pinnacle of all ages. We believed him too. Xavier had long, well-kept dreadlocks that ended where his shoulders started and were always in place no matter how wild he got.

Percy and I were both sixteen. We had both been born in July and both been named after our fathers. We even looked alike, both sporting medium-length nappy hair; people often made the mistake of thinking we were fraternal twins.

Old Boy was without question my best friend. I was never mad at Old Boy. We argued with each other more often than with anyone else, but I was never mad at him. From Cedric's memory, I recalled him only getting mad at me one time in six years. We were two peas in a pod, two left shoes, just falling short of one whole person.

Our little band skipped school all the time. We would all go over to Old Boy's house for some rest and relaxation. Now as I said, Old Boy was the youngest—he was fifteen years old—and although Percy and I were only a year older, we felt much smarter than him. In many ways, we were. Xavier, Percy, and I all had our faults, but up until that point, we had been smart enough to avoid involvement in gangs. Old Boy thought it would be cool to make some money and run a grow house for one of the local gangs. As his friends, we had all advised against it, but once the money started rolling in, we only opened our mouths to catch a spare quarter. I guess that was what a small amount of wealth would do to a man at a young age. Because Old Boy had the money, we spent most of our time doing what he wanted.

Every day after the bell rang, or after we decided we'd had enough, we went over to Old Boy's grow house to smoke. Old Boy lived with his older brother, who was always out gangbanging or finding some way to get into trouble. This meant that we had a house to ourselves. Old Boy had become quite good at growing marijuana through repetition. Terrible with numbers at school, he was good with them when it came to managing the product. This meant that he always adjusted his numbers to allow us as much free smoke as possible.

The goods were set up in Old Boy's attic, so we would all go to the basement and smoke in a circle. Well, one day we were doing just that, smoking in a circle, when Percy became quiet. Xavier held a blunt in between his fingers and sucked hungrily at one end. When he had satisfied his want, he held out his hand to Old Boy, who then passed it to Percy, who didn't partake in it himself. If I hadn't been high out of my mind, I would've noticed this as cause for alarm.

Old Boy's basement was aptly decorated with all sorts of drug-related tchotchkes, things he had ordered online, which served as playful innuendos to his criminalist craft. The marijuana had made these trinkets extremely notable to me. I settled my attention on a bobble-head of an underground rapper with a blunt placed appropriately in his mouth. I didn't notice Percy's distantness until the thing that caused it exploded out of him. I slowly snapped out of my trance. The basement had become a sauna from our exhaust. Xavier and Old Boy were talking about some meaningless thing. I think it had been about a girl named Stephanie, and they were arguing over which one of them she liked better. I couldn't remember Stephanie being interested in either one of them. Percy had only acquired a secondhand high and was the soberest.

"What's the matter with you?" I asked innocently enough.

He didn't move, and I saw a scowl where a smile usually was. I got up from the couch I was sitting on and nudged him lightly.

I was not expecting him to clock me square in the face.

He had done it quickly. His knuckles knew exactly where to go to do the maximum damage. Xavier and Old Boy stopped their conversation. By the looks on their faces, you would've thought Percy had gotten up and hit them too. I fell back clear over the couch and onto the floor. I tried to get on my feet as soon as I hit the ground, but that was a dumb move because I stumbled into the wall and ripped one of Old Boy's weed posters into oblivion.

"What the—aye, c'mon, man, watch that," he said.

I slid down against the wall in defeat. There was no way I was going to regain my balance in my influenced state.

"Ya pops some kind of man!" Percy yelled.

Through my eyes, I could see a colorful onrush of everything there was to see in that room, psychedelic and obnoxious, but my ears were unaffected, so I listened.

"Look at you. I bet you don't even know. Tell your pops that if he ever come near my mamma again, he'll get more than what you just got!"

He exited up the steps, stomping with his baggy jeans a'swishing. The door slammed, and that was that.

After the incident at Old Boy's grow house, I went home. The high wore off quickly, and all the fun had been stripped out of the basement along with my friendship with Old Boy. We lived in a bungalow on the edge of our troublesome neighborhood. It was a tiny little thing, but it was cozy. It radiated any heat you threw into it—love, hate, and actual heat. I was on autopilot as soon as I left the grow house. I made my way in the general direction of my abode until I spotted its low roof barely peeking above similar houses. The screen door was only partially attached to the frame, but I swung it open hard and twisted the knob.

Josiah was the only one in the house. He was sitting on the couch, laptop in tow making beats. He recognized my frustration.

"What now?" he asked. He set his laptop down on the center table and got up. "Was it Lamarr again?"

Percy hadn't hit me hard enough to leave a noticeable mark.

"Nah, it wasn't that," Josiah concluded on his own. "You ain't bruised."

He sat back down and repositioned his laptop. It was funny; he didn't look like any of my other siblings, yet he looked so much like me, only older. He had a strap of stubble about his jawline that I had failed to obtain even in this life. His nose was pierced like a bull's. He had laugh lines but never laughed.

"I got in a fight," I informed him.

He kept his focus on the screen in front of him.

"With Percy," I said, regaining his attention.

"Percy? What you go and fight Percy for?" he asked.

"I didn't do a thing but kick it with Old Boy and them. He's the one that up and punched me half to sleep," I said.

"That don't sound like no Percy I know," Josiah said.

He wanted more, but I wasn't going to legitimize Percy's accusations by mentioning them.

"I don't know, Jo" was all I replied.

"Yo ass better find out and fix things up with him. He been with you since day one. Y'all too close to be fighting like that."

Josiah went back to work on his sonic recipe, clicking away at some sound wave, chiseling away its imperfections. When he wasn't doing something stupid, he worked at his computer, making music for his aspiring rapper friends. He had sold drugs, stolen phones, his clothes, you name it, all to buy a laptop and mixing software last Christmas.

I remembered last Christmas like it was yesterday, even though it was before my time. We hadn't been able to afford much; our family was always on a financial strain. We were like those bugs that always fell into pools and then struggled to find the edge only to fall back in when a wave hit them. Money had always been an elusive. We said we didn't need it, but that was because we didn't have it. We said people who had it didn't need it, and the people who had it couldn't fathom why we didn't just make more. They lived up there and us down here in the humdrum hemisphere lacking in glamour, grit in exchange for survival; those were the rules for us. We weren't submerged, but parts of us were.

Percy had claimed that my father had violated the trust of my mother by having relations with his mother. I knew this. I understood the accusation and what it meant quite well, but I didn't want to know it. I had half expected not to care, but when you inherited someone's life, you also inherited the things dear to them—their emotional investments, some of their fears. The relationship of Cedric Burgan's parents was mine to cherish.

I conjured up whatever obligatory naïveté was needed to bury my understanding, but Cedric's memories were too clear. I knew. I knew he had cheated on her before. I knew he said he had changed. I knew Percy's mom was beautiful and lonesome as she had told me herself when I visited him. I knew about the absence of fathers. I knew, but I didn't want to know. I would've given anything not to know.

My mother now was a jumpy woman. She worried often and about things that were out of her control. My father was yet another thing that she could not control. He was a hardy, strong-willed man who did as he pleased even when compromise was the smarter option. Their occupations didn't define them, but they did adhere to their personalities. She assisted nurses, constantly worrying about patients who would be out in a week or the ones there was no hope for.

He was a stone-faced factory worker who made car parts and drank when he wasn't almost losing a hand—not that he didn't drink during work.

After taking a few sips of soda in the fridge, I went to my room and thought about the accusation even though I didn't want to think about it. I knew. I knew that it was true. Once when my father dropped me off at Percy's house, he looked at my friend's mother with the same lustful look that I myself had whenever a girl from school would whisper in my ear and the aroma of her bubblegum tickled my nose. I gave him the benefit of the doubt then. I put it out of my mind in favor of better thoughts. Now it had come back, and this time, it couldn't leave my mind.

My creaky door was closed, and I had the loud ceiling fan running even though it was cold in case anyone tried to listen to me think. On my bed, I looked up at the faint rosettes carved into the ceiling. Why was it his fault? I found myself asking this question. Sure he had betrayed the trust of my mother again. Sure he had ruined whatever sanctity was left in their matrimony. Sure he had put his urges on top of our family, but she had done the same, Percy's mom. Lucille White. Brown skinned and black hearted, she did this. She seduced him. As I stared at the ceiling, a warmth in my stomach pulsated; anger was brewing. She was my mother's friend. Surely their friendship held comparable weight to marriage. My other father could have had several wives; most of the village had found it strange that he did not. He had said that my mother was worth all the wives in the world, and that was that. Why couldn't that exist now?

"Have you no shame, Lucille?" I thought.

I told myself whatever I needed to hear to justify my newfound hatred for her. How could she think that she could just disrupt my already-disrupted life? She must've flashed her slightly crooked teeth or batted her barren, incomplete lashes. Her imperfections had been just perfect enough for him to risk everything. A divorce would mean even less of what we already had little of. A divorce would mean Josiah would have to start making money in dangerously creative ways. A divorce would mean no family for me. The elders had gifted me a second life, and I would not lose my family a second time.

I knew. I knew that I hated Lucille and Percy White and that I loved my brother—that much I knew.

XVII

I stopped seeing Percy. When we all wanted to hang out, I would check to see if he was included. He did the same thing, and when it became apparent that, for whatever reason, our friend group preferred me over him, he stopped talking to us.

I saw Lucille one day while Old Boy and I were out shoplifting. It was Old Boy's idea to let me in on one of his favorite illegal pastimes (of which he had many). Shoplifting was a sport to him. I had refused at first; it wasn't my style. I didn't *have* a style. I had waited to be hit with an interesting personality like one waited for puberty…it never came.

Old Boy was young, stupid, and itching to be a menace. He convinced me to be his partner in crime. We were in a grocery store of all places. He chose it because it was the store closest to our school, and I followed along because I was hungry and didn't want to eat mom's cobbler for the sixtieth day in a row.

In hindsight, that grocery store was a shoplifter's dream—old cameras, careless employees…heck, I doubted the RFID scanners in the alarms still worked. So many prospects, so many aisles without eyes, and what did I decide to steal? Magic Markers—not even the twenty-four pack. They were in a bin filled with miscellaneous items, insignificant things, and knickknacks. Old Boy was more ambitious: a small box of cupcakes in the baked goods section.

"See that guy over there, Cedric?" Old Boy pointed out vaguely.

I scanned around until I found the person at the end of his finger. "Yeah, I see him," I replied.

He was a skinny fellow. His ear buds rattled against his lobes as he leaned lazily over the checkout counter of the baked goods section. He let his mandatory off-blue apron hang off the edge of the counter, partially covering the plump English muffins that were on display so that only the top-heavy outlines could be seen through the sapphire curtain.

"Normally that guy would be in charge of making sure people like me don't steal by keeping an eye on everything, but Mr. Employee of the Month is preoccupied," Old Boy said.

I almost laughed, but this was out of my comfort zone by far. Old Boy studied the employee before fixing his eyes on a rack right next to the counter. On that rack were enough boxed chocolate cupcakes to feed a sugar-toothed shark. Old Boy was foolhardy but still afraid of his older brother, so he went for a single box in hopes of decreasing his likeliness of getting caught and, by extension, getting an earful. He was swift. Before I could open my mouth to object for what must've been the thousandth time, he was off. He didn't run; in fact, his upkeep of normality was what cloaked him. He walked so inconspicuously right next to Mr. Employee of the Month. The man didn't even bother to look up. Quickly, in a matter of seconds, he plucked the box from the shelf and walked toward me with the muffins hidden beneath his arm.

I never liked the idea of stealing, and I never liked it when I was stolen from, but I found something tempting about it. The taboo sent a rush through me. The rush made the hairs on my neck reach for the stars, the hairs yelled at my blood to run, my blood obeyed, and my veins didn't deny. All of a sudden, I started seeing how one might let something like this develop into a pastime. As Old Boy walked hurriedly toward me and motioned for me to follow, I became infatuated with the idea of taking what the world had decided we were not privy to have.

We were interrupted by the sudden sight of my mother, who had arrived to buy groceries along with her friend Lucille White. They had been hoping to buy some vegetables, probably for a stew, and had decided they'd be more successful as a joint venture. We were in the aisle for cereal boxes, and Old Boy had been the one to point them out to me.

"Goddamn it, it's Ms. White and your mamma. I better bounce."

He tossed his acquired bounty into an entirely new section of the store ruled by loops, flakes, and wheats. I didn't have time to object, so I nodded off a silent good-bye and headed toward my mother. Seeing Old Boy and I together would have revealed to her that we were up to no good.

I could hide my agenda, but I couldn't hide my dislike for Ms. White. I felt a lump form in my throat as she spotted me, smiled, and went in for a hug. It amazed me how women could be so discreet with their sabotage. Here a woman who had been responsible for putting my parents' marriage in harm's way was hugging me as if she hadn't nearly destroyed my family. I couldn't take it.

"My, Cedric, how you've grown!" she said in that high-pitched overdone way that told me I hadn't really grown at all.

She strengthened her grip around me, but I stayed limp. I couldn't bear her embrace.

"Cedric, what's the matter with you? Hug Ms. White," my mother scolded.

"I'm not feeling well. Wouldn't want her to catch something," I faked.

"Oh, it's all right. He a man now. He ain't up for hugging. Ain't that right, Cedric?" Ms. White teased.

I felt like punching her, but that would've been crossing the line, even for my temper. I was faced with a dilemma. The two women looked at me; I saw the cluelessness of my mother and the insincerity of the person she called her friend. Without waiting for either one of them to say another word, I turned around and walked out of the store. I heard one of them calling me—or both of them; I wasn't paying attention. I just kept walking until I saw the door to our old Jeep. I walked until the parking lot it was parked in could fit in the palm of my hand. I walked until my neighborhood, my homeland, surrounded me and comforted me—all of it, the pits that barked angrily behind weak chain-link fences, the bottles in soggy paper bags too big for the storm drains, the boarded-up windows, the sirens, there were always sirens, the smell of metal and decay, of poverty, of home, of everything.

When my mother finally did come home with the groceries, she was furious. She yelled at me, slapped me, hit me, and cursed at me for embarrassing her in front of one of her friends.

She did everything in her power to punish me, but I didn't say a word back to her. My words were loaded, and any one of them might've killed her.

Percy's mom had been offended, and I guess she must have voiced her offense to her son, because after school the next day, when I was walking home, I felt a foot press against my side. Before I knew what was happening, I was on the ground. Out of an alleyway, two figures came out and stood next to me. I recognized the loud colors on the shoes that started kicking me as being a trademark for Lamarr, but the person doing most of the talking was Percy.

"You think you can disrespect my mamma like that, nigga? Huh? Huh!"

Points of pain then popped up from all around my body as they kicked me.

"You just like your daddy, ain't you? What? Was she the one that cheated on your mamma?" Percy screamed.

His kicks were getting harder. I adjusted myself to allow for my backpack to absorb the hardest blows.

"Shut up!" I screamed back.

They kicked me a few more times before they got bored or their legs got tired; I didn't know which happened first. Then they ran away as I spat out blood. Dazed and barely able to walk, I stumbled home. The pain put a damper on my speed, so I knew I wouldn't make it home as early as I usually did.

Our neighborhood was riddled with gas stations and liquor stores, and at the center of it was a park too dangerous to be of any use as a park. Mainly drug deals would go down there, and we would hear about these drug deals but only when they went bad and made the news. I would collapse if I took the long way home, so I decided to cut through the park. As it got dark, virtually no one else was around. I didn't come by a single person on my way home. I didn't know whether that was good or bad, but I assumed it was good because I felt like Good Samaritans were few and far between in my world, and I would sooner come across a mugger who would take advantage of my injured state. Our house did have a fence, and to my dismay, when I came across it, the gate was closed.

The lock to open it was always cumbersome. I knew I didn't have the strength. I tossed my backpack over and then tossed myself over. I caught the sharp end of a picket and then slid over it. Two hard slaps on the back door and some waiting produced an open door with Josiah in the frame.

Everything went hazy then.

Josiah talked on the phone with someone.

I struggled to stay conscious.

His voice sounded dense as if it was being filtered through glass.

I lay down on the couch.

He was next to me talking softly.

I closed my eyes.

I got hurt.

He got his coat.

I didn't move.

He darted off, angry and ready for war.

I had a fractured rib. My torso was covered with bruises and cuts. I woke up on a hospital bed that was placed in the cleanest room I had ever seen. The air felt purified, and the floor showed my reflection when I looked at it. Witt was sitting on the bed when I came to.

"How much is all this going to cost?" I asked.

He smiled. I'd never seen him tired before, but for the first time I noticed how much older he was.

"Don't worry about that. I took care of it."

I tried to get up.

"Don't get up."

He held his hand to my forehead and felt around. This was the second time I was in a hospital, but this time there was a face missing.

"Where's Jo?" I asked.

Witt looked down at his shoes. "In jail," he said quietly.

"What?"

I tried to get up again. Everything hurt.

"Goddamn it, I told you not to get up." He scratched his head. "Well, technically he's in holding."

"What did he do?"

Witt chuckled. "If you have to ask, then you don't know him that well."

I knew what he meant. I remembered Josiah's thousand-yard panther stare, the kind only a man on a mission had. I remembered how he had walked out of the door. He took long, powerful strides.

"Did he kill anyone?" I asked.

"No, thank God," Witt replied.

"Good."

"He gave those two boys quite the beating though."

"Really?" I asked.

"Oh yeah, I bet they'd give anything to have your injuries. I've seen Jo beat people up before, but this time is different. He really outdid himself. They got him on assault charges."

"How much is bail?" I asked.

"A lot."

I looked at him expectantly. I hated to ask, but it wasn't as though we had any other choice.

Sensing that I was about to beg, Witt shook his head. "Cedric, if I could've posted bail, I would have. I know the drill by now. It's different this time. This judge knows Josiah by name. She also thinks that I'm his get-out-of-jail-free card, thanks to Barnaby."

"Who?" I asked.

"Boyd Barnaby. There're a lot good cops in the world, but the one who was in the courtroom was Boyd Barnaby. I think Percy went to him because he knows Officer Barnaby's got it out for your brother. The man hates his guts. Anyway, he made the argument that I shouldn't be allowed to post Jo's bail because I've done it every single time, leading to Jo having no repercussions. He claims I'm funding Jo's 'urban terrorism,' whatever that means."

"So what then? He just goes to jail?" I said.

Witt shrugged. "Cedric, my hands are tied, and as much as I hate to admit, Officer Barnaby was really convincing. The bail's still there, but the judge said the money can't come from me in any way, shape, or form."

"I can probably scrape some money together," I said.

"Look, Jo's a repeat offender. The only reason he didn't get hard time right off the bat is because of you. The lawyer I got him made the case that he was acting out to protect you, and it just barely worked."

"How much is bail?" I asked.

"He's a repeat offender."

"Witt, how much is bail?"

He was silent for a moment, thinking, as if saying it the right way might take away from the hopelessness of the situation.

"Five thousand dollars."

To the right person, five thousand dollars was not a lot of money. It was only a thousand once and then four more times; a thousand was only ten one hundreds. And how much was a hundred dollars really? I wasn't the right person. I wasn't Witt. This Officer Barnaby had single-handedly cut off our lifeline. It was sad how a few digits could mean the difference between possible and impossible for people who were all supposed to be worth the same. Possible or not, I would earn every penny. Somehow.

"I know they jumped you, but tell me what would've happened if they hadn't, if it was just one of them and they wanted to start something?" Witt said.

"I would pummel them," I answered truthfully. I made a fist and struck hard at a mock assailant.

"You could just walk away," Witt suggested as he kicked a pebble. It skidded across the sidewalk and stopped just a few feet ahead of us.

"I can never walk away, you know that," I said.

It was a calm Saturday morning, and only a few children were brave enough to play at the local park.

The parents of our area only let a few of their children out to play at a time. I didn't understand the purpose of this until I overheard my mother say one time that it was a precautionary measure. If things were to go bad between the gangs, then parents wouldn't lose all their children at once. She had said this while talking to Josiah, who had asked her.

After she told him the reason, he replied, "Like not putting all your eggs in one basket."

Most of the residents hadn't woken up, and so Witt thought it was a good idea to go for a walk with me. I was well enough to walk now. A doctor's note scribbled out in hasty, sophisticated handwriting had given me leave from school for a while. I healed quickly. My recovery was expedited by warm blankets and steaming bowls of chicken noodle soup, the taste hiding the natural bitterness of the powerful medicine, which my mom inserted carefully in my meals.

Not wanting to tell my mother about Percy, Witt had said that I fell down his staircase while over at his house. As for why Josiah was in jail, all we said was that he beat up some very bad people. She knew we weren't telling her the whole truth, but she bought into the lie. It shielded her from having knowledge of the decayed childhood relationships she held dear, and it cast her troublesome baby in a noble light. All was well.

"Why we gotta keep talking about me anyway?" I asked.

Suddenly, Witt got a running start and kicked the pebble so hard that it flew straight off the sidewalk and rested in a bed of leaves under a nearby tree. He grumbled some unidentifiable thing under his breath.

"I used to be like him," he said.

I looked at him doubtfully. Witt smiled.

"Well, really I was more like you. I don't know if anybody can be as out of control as he is or if anyone can get into trouble like he does."

We continued walking.

"If Pete were here, he'd kill him for getting locked up," Witt said.

"Pete isn't here," I said.

"He always hoped that Jo would stay out of trouble. You know, he could never bear the thought of him rotting away in some cell. He tried to get me to take Jo under my wing back when I had just gotten into money and Jo was younger and not so hardheaded."

I laughed. "How did that work out?"

Witt smiled. Bigger this time. "I was too busy back then, too self-centered. I was like, 'Sure, sure,' but I never had any plans of really trying to keep him out of trouble. Maybe if I had, things would be different now."

"I doubt it," I said.

"What did Pete think of me?" Witt asked after a moment.

I smirked. "What kind of question was that?" I thought about it.

"He idolized you; you were his best friend. I mean not many people get to start where we come from and turn into something. It's like those arcade machines where a little ball falls down a bunch of pegs and it's gotta land in the right slot for the prize."

"Pachinko?"

"Pachinko."

"Let me ask you another question."

I rolled my eyes. I had had just about enough of his questions. These days I was the one always asking him questions; it was never the other way around. There was something about a person whom your older brother looked up to, like how you were surprised the first time you found out your parents had parents of their own. It made you think your grandparents knew everything, including stuff your parents didn't. Thing was, I couldn't remember Witt being wrong about anything, ever.

"All right, ask away," I permitted.

"How many black people from around here you see in college?"

At that, I rolled my eyes hard enough for my brain to come into view. I had expected something less like a lecture.

"What? You don't like that question? Is it too easy? Answer it then."

The sky became increasingly lit, and one by one, the doors on the houses of the neighborhood opened unpredictably. It would almost always be a child who exited the house, never an adult, not this early.

"Only one of y'all at the park at a time!"

A rule that only the parents, Josiah, and I knew the reasoning behind it.

"Don't put all your eggs in one casket."

I scanned the streets surrounding the park, hoping to see Xavier or Old Boy or a lesser friend who hadn't yet lost my favor. When I didn't see anyone, I returned my attention to Witt, who had been waiting patiently for my well-thought-out response.

"I don't know. I guess not that many," I answered.

"Not that many, right. I know you're getting letters from colleges. You know firsthand how much money all that cost. Your old man couldn't even get you that video game system you wanted," Witt continued.

"Yeah, the new one that just came out," I responded, searching for a clue as to where he was going. He didn't have to rub it in.

"Yeah, the new one," he said. "How many people around here you think can afford school?"

"Not that many," I answered.

"How many people around here you think would go to school if they could?"

I shrugged. "Around here hardly anyone finishes high school."

"And that's 'cause they didn't have anyone to push them...let alone a chance to begin with, without all that extra clutter in their lives."

He had lost me.

"By poverty. By friends doing shit that's no good for anyone. By home lives in places that don't feel like home. By this life I was lucky enough to escape," he clarified.

We both turned around and started back home when we saw that Breaux Street was in proximity.

"My point is you have actual opportunity. If Percy wants to mess around with that lawless hoodlum, then fine, but I don't want to watch you slip away too," he said.

"Why on earth would I?" I objected.

"Not saying that you want to, but I talked with Percy's mom, and she told me that Lamarr's ways had a way of sneaking up on her boy."

A shiver ran up my spine at the mention of Percy's mother.

"You're a fighter. I know that, you know that, but you can't get involved because of school. You know their intentions now, so they won't catch you off guard again. I'm just tellin' you, revenge isn't worth it. You got so much more to be, so much more to do in this world. I'm talking about you, Cedric. You got so much potential. You half-ass your way through school and get the grades that I struggled to get. I want you to understand that me and you have a chance at something," he finished.

We walked back to my house. Witt phoned himself a ride and went back to the paradise of Palmstock Court. I spent the rest of the day inside until my mother's return from work indicated that supper would be ready soon. My father was out late, drinking with some of his work buddies.

My mother and I had chicken and mashed potatoes for supper. It tasted as good as always. A river of gravy separated two high masses of white. I dug my spoon into the ravine. The clinking of metal against glass was the only sound. She didn't make small talk with me. If she spoke, we would realize how empty the table was and that the two of us alone were not enough to carry a conversation. Beside our hands and plates of food, there rested a single sloppily opened letter on the table meant for Jo. It was from the Bangers & Bops record company. Their message didn't take more than a third of a page, but what was in it was enough to change Jo's life forever. They had seen a jump in artists hop-ing to be signed by them. Some of them were legitimately talented, most were nothing special, but the best ones had the same thing in common; they had all gotten their instrumentals from Jo. They wanted him to work for them as a paid intern. When my mother had read that short heartbreaking sentence, it took the color from her face.

I took it upon myself to wash the dishes. A scheme bubbled up in my head; the cleansing of china egged it on. In the kitchen through thin walls, I heard weeping. It was muffled, but I could still make out the sniffling, the patchy pitches, the momentary instances where it ceased—failed attempts at composure. The limits of my mother had been reached.

My fists itched, and it had nothing to do with the soapy water my hands were in.

XVIII

Prior to the villainy of Lucille and Percy White, there was one person who deserved all my hate—Lamarr Longman. He was my age and protected by a horde of gangbangers, having risen through the ranks to become somewhat of a leader. Their gang was most prominent in the southern part of town. There was another gang in the north part of the town and another gang with so few numbers that they were barely recognized, mainly made up of ex-convicts drifting out of a larger city. Some of the people who hung around him were from that same city. Why they would subject themselves to the orders of someone as young as me was beyond my understanding.

Lamarr Longman had a head that was shaped like an emaciated jellybean. He was completely bald and not by choice either. He couldn't grow a single hair on his head. I think it was hereditary because people said that his father couldn't grow hair...that was back when his father was still around. Lamarr possessed the innate ability to piss off anyone he wanted to with ease, although it was almost always me that he pissed off.

He came from a troubled home—not that that made him special. Most of my friends came from imperfect homes, but Lamarr's was what you might have called exceptionally troubled. When his father left his family when Lamarr was less than a year old, the resulting pressure had caused Lamarr's mother to spiral into intense and seemingly incurable alcoholism, which inevitably led to her dying of alcohol poisoning when Lamarr was six. He then went on to be raised by his uncle Darius, who, with the number of children already dependent on him in addition to his unstable relationship with one of the local gangs, was in no position to raise another child. Lamarr was taken in but completely ignored, and whatever trauma was inside him grew.

Just a few years back, an event had changed the tone of the town. Darius's house had been raided by some thugs, and everyone in it, all eleven of his children, were gunned down. Nobody knew what gang the thugs belonged to, only that Darius had gotten on their bad side. Nobody knew how the gang members had found Darius's house either. It was well known that Darius had got involved with the gangs but also well known that he'd gone through great lengths to keep his home hidden. When the police arrived at the scene, they found enough evidence to pin down one suspect, a notorious drug pusher from outside of town. There was a particularly nasty rumor that circulated around about my enemy that for a long time I had thought to be too evil to be true, even for him. It had been too detailed though and had too many witnesses and not enough naysayers for it to be false. It was well known that Lamarr had an unsteady relationship with his uncle.

Apparently, Lamarr's uncle owed some loan sharks an obscene amount of money, and when the loan sharks sent out their men to teach Lamarr's uncle a lesson, Lamarr himself had told them where his uncle lived. The men rushed into the house, spraying everything they saw with bullets. When they found that Darius wasn't among the dead, they went back to Lamarr. Having no idea that a slew of his cousins had just been murdered, Lamarr told them of a second location. Darius had gone to a motel so that if any trouble were to happen, his children wouldn't be caught in the crosshairs (it was in a Murphy's Motel, a local hideout that held more than its fair share of druggies and self-proclaimed outlaws). The men, with the blood of his cousins still on their hands, had told him that they were just going to rough up his uncle and not do any real damage. Clouded by his disdain for his uncle, Lamarr believed them.

When the men found the motel room and knocked on the door, Lamarr's uncle had, for some reason, answered it with a knife in his hand. He would have been killed anyway, but this led to his death being more immediate. He was shot twice in the chest and died in the doorway of his room. In return for giving away his uncle's location, the men had given Lamarr some money, which he used to buy himself a new pair of shoes. When word spread of how coldhearted he was and how much he didn't give a fuck, well, Lamarr used the newfound image to his own advantage.

So he became a dark and slender boss who wore large, expensive clothes that complemented his ruthlessly expensive lifestyle. All for the very low price of a dozen blood tokens.

As for why he and I clashed so hard, I did not know. We both had come from broken homes, but he lived a broken life; I didn't.

I wasn't like that. Jo wasn't like that. We were different.

We had a family that worked and provided for us, and this was no secret. Maybe that was why he hated me, and maybe the reason I hated him back was because with the way things were going, I might slowly turn into him. It had started off small when we were small—a few words exchanged on the playground, a teasing name that we didn't fully understand the meaning of, only that it hurt the other. As we grew, our conflict grew too. He lost his innocence quicker than I did, so he had been the first to escalate our fights; from words to punches, the transition was quick. I could credit numerous suspensions to him and even more scars. I didn't expect to see Percy by his side during school the next day.

I had been on my way to my first class of the day. I didn't believe my eyes at first; I had to do a double take. That was when I realized that our friendship was really over—when Percy had stooped so low as to partner with my worst enemy.

I didn't ask Xavier to talk to him for me, but being the good friend that he was, he did. Xavier told me that not only had Percy joined forces with Lamarr, but he had also been initiated into Lamarr's gang. This was the main message, but it was hidden underneath an array of profanities and insults. I didn't care much, but secretly I was concerned for Percy. Lamarr's gang was no joke, and neither were the deaths that stemmed from their violence.

I had a knack for English, and biology was not English. Sometimes I felt as though the second hand on a clock took a few ticks back when you weren't looking. I checked again; it hadn't moved, or if it had, it was barely at all. Mr. Graham talked on about the components of a cell. I liked science but not enough to stay interested for the whole forty-five minutes we had it. I looked around the room; laminated posters of skeletal systems and definitions for biology terms dotted the walls. I was on the third story of our school, and the fact that I had a window seat that presented the distractions of the outdoors made it very difficult for me to keep focus. I slowly moved my eyes to take a look.

My teacher was very aware as to who was paying attention and who wasn't. If even one person said the quietest comment while he was talking, he would stop immediately and give everyone in the room a hard time. I didn't want to be caught daydreaming. Besides, at least for this unit, I actually knew most of the stuff.

The tops of the trees took up most of the viewing space, but they were a sight to see themselves. A squirrel ran through the branches on the tree closest to me. It stopped and sniffed the air before turning to face me. Its ears twitched as it studied me. Even the darkest and beadiest eyes could reveal something. The ones on the squirrel's face seemed unsure, as if it was nervous about something. The fur on its back pricked up as a shiver ran the length of its body. Then as if our brief meeting had never happened, it turned around and bounded to the next treetop. From there, it scurried down the trunk and approached the street as if on a mission. I turned my head to try to regain focus on the discussion, and then I heard the sharp sound of wheels swerving. I turned back just quickly enough to see the back of a taxi recentering in its lane, leaving a sheet of squirrel behind.

Mission or no mission, tires couldn't tell.

Its pressed body now lifeless, I watched, as other cars flattened it more; next to it were a few other pieces of debris, either flattened or waiting to be. I liked animals, so watching a squirrel die wasn't very fun, but like the death of the messenger or the demise of the blackbird, memories that seemed so faint to me they felt more like dreams, I couldn't look away.

"Cedric, are you paying attention?" I heard a voice ask.

I looked up to see Mr. Graham staring me down. I had a bad habit of disappointing Mr. Graham because he had taught my brother, who had been a surprisingly good student, and, sadly, I was not my brother. I answered with a quick nod. He watched me for a few seconds and then turned back around to resume his lesson. I didn't want to look outside again. There were only a few minutes left of class, but for some reason, time didn't want to proceed. I looked around the classroom again. People were zoning out left and right, and their attempts to hide it were pathetic. This was the last class of the day, and everyone was

anxious for it to be over. Xavier had suggested that I skip with him—
we could have done bad and fun things—but I had worse on my mind.
I resorted to looking at the woodwork of my desk as the excruciatingly
boring minutes passed by. Mr. Graham passed out the homework, and
I slipped mine into my book bag. He looked at me.

"No one should be packing up. We still have two minutes in class."

Before then, I was trying to be polite, but I couldn't numb my irritation any longer.

"But it's almost time to leave, and the bell is about to ring," I stated.

Mr. Graham smiled pompously. "The bell doesn't dismiss you,
Cedric. I do."

His uptightness angered me.

"Then why the fuck did the school go through all the trouble in-
stalling a bell system in the building?"

Everyone in the classroom stared at me.

Did you ever get that feeling when you knew you shouldn't do
something, but you did it anyway on impulse and then regretted it immediately afterward? That was the feeling I had.

Mr. Graham's body was unresponsive, his hands carried on with
writing, I almost thought he hadn't heard me. The loud ringing of the
bell broke the awkward silence.

"Cedric, don't forget to get your detention on your way out," he
said.

I got a few empathetic looks from my peers as I made my way over
to him and grabbed the bright-yellow slip with my name on it.

"That's fifteen minutes of my life that I'm never going to get back,"
I murmured to myself as I was about to walk out.

I decided that since I had a decent amount of time before I had to
get home, it would probably be best to serve it now. Detention was
always boring as hell; I knew that well enough. I stopped before leaving
out the door and turned around. I gave Mr. Graham my yellow slip and

sat down at a desk. It was only fifteen minutes; it wouldn't take very much time so long as the clock didn't hit me with any more shady maneuvers. Mr. Graham pulled out a worksheet and placed it on my desk.

"What do you want me to do with this?" I asked.

"Fill out to the best of your ability. You have a D in this class. You've shown promise on some of the newer material, but I would still like to assess your knowledge on the subjects we will be covering."

I raised my eyebrows as I scanned the first page. It was asking me about things like how insulin worked and when was the best time for it to be used; it had questions about the effects of adrenaline and other hormones and even a question about things that stimulated brain cells. I knew none of this, and I doubted I could get the answers right. I gave him a doubtful look.

"It might not be graded if you try hard enough," he offered.

"*Might* not be graded?" I asked. It was the best I was going to get.

Mr. Graham sat back at his desk and took a sip of his afternoon coffee. "I suggest you get to work, and, Cedric..." he said.

I faced him, trying my hardest not to roll my eyes.

"I want you to try. You have potential. Don't waste it."

I wondered if Mr. Graham knew who Witt was.

After school, the first thing on my mind was getting to Old Boy's house. When I got to his house, I knocked twice quickly on the door. When Old Boy opened it, I could see the top of Xavier's head descending the steps that led to the basement.

"We thought you wasn't gonna show!" Old Boy greeted.

He turned around to follow Xavier. He was carrying a hookah in his hand that'd been decorated with tiny paper cutouts of our favorite artists taped to the body. I closed the door behind me and tapped him on the back, interrupting him before he could completely bring the hookah to his mouth.

"I need to ask you something," I said.

Without hesitation, Old Boy handed me the hookah. "It's all yours," he said with a smile.

"Nah, nah." I handed the thing back to him. "I was wondering if you couldn't hook me up with the crew that you run with," I said.

His smile got wider. "You want to join North Gang?" he asked.

I nodded. "They do pay well, don't they?"

He nodded.

"Jo's in jail again," I said.

"Witt?" he asked.

"Not this time. Some cop has it out for Jo, and he convinced the judge to make Witt stay out of it," I explained.

Old Boy shook his head. "That's fucked up. Well, if you sure you want in, you gonna have to talk to Slicker. He the one in charge a' newcomers."

He wrapped his lips around the mouthpiece of the hookah and sucked in hard. Smoke danced out of his slightly parted lips as well as his round dark nostrils. An aroma of chocolate and mint filled Old Boy's nearly empty living room.

"You can take me to him, right?" I asked.

Old Boy sighed before taking another lazy sip from the mouthpiece. "Let's get lit real quick, and then we can go," he offered.

"I don't want to get there too late though. Can't we leave now? There'll be weed there probably," I begged.

"Oh shit!" he said all of a sudden. "Good looking out, Cedric. I almost forgot."

He walked over into his narrow hallway, motioning for me to follow. On the ceiling, in the middle of the hallway, there was a rectangular indentation with a long brown rope dangling from it. The rope dangled just above our heads. Old Boy reached for it and pulled. A ladder slid from the indentation, and the first step was right before our feet. Old Boy was the first to climb up, and I followed.

The first thing I felt was the intense heat of the attic, partially due to a lack of air conditioning but also because there were numerous rows of high-power lights. The whole space was blinding. The musky scent of marijuana was overpowering and concentrated. I had left the hookah in Old Boy's living room to his disappointment because apparently being near the product made him want to take a hit. The floor of the attic protested against my being on it by making hideous and unnerving creaking noises with every nervous step I took. The wood looked weak enough to collapse at any moment. The rest of the setup was comparatively well put together. The UV lights couldn't have been more than a few months old, the clear bins that the plants grew in were thick and sturdy, and even the plants themselves were equidistantly placed apart and neat. All on the floor, I counted twenty-five bins, five by five, each one holding ten or so plants. In a dark corner was a watering can that must've been heavy because Old Boy grunted loudly when he lifted it. He walked along the rows, sprinkling each bin with water as he went. The floor beneath us shrieked angrily. I wondered what it would look like if we were to fall through, plants and all. Old Boy had no authority figures in his life except for his brother, who visited about as often as aliens and almost never disciplined him. How would he have reacted? I could see it: Old Boy with the watering can over his head, me in a beanbag chair made entirely of dirt, the smell of old oak, dusty insulation, and weed wafting down into the basement. If that sound didn't make Xavier come up, the smell certainly would.

"All right, you ready to go?" Old Boy asked, breaking me away from my thoughts.

"Yeah," I answered.

We climbed down the ladder. Old Boy kicked its base, sending it retreating back into where it came, and with that we set out. Old Boy told Xavier that we were going out. Xavier sighed but ultimately looked as though he couldn't have cared less where we went. I attributed his nonchalance to what must've been that *eighteen cool* he had, cooler than the mint in Old Boy's hookah tobacco, cooler than Lucille White's ice-cold heart—that age was the age to be.

XIX

When we entered Slicker's house, which was just down the street, there was a festive ambience, a kind of cordiality that told me that everyone in that house was *eighteen cool*. People were sleeping on the floor. I didn't understand how anyone could be inert in such a wild place. Loud music with baselines that thumped the core of me, even more so than the beating of my own heart, played continuously. The sleeping people were out of our way, so we didn't have to exercise caution to walk over them. Old Boy led me to the living room. People walked around aimlessly and without purpose with cups filled with bright liquids held closely in their hands.

"Is there a party going on?" I asked, my voice barely able to be heard over the music.

"It's always like this!" Old Boy replied.

In the living room were some guys sitting around a coffee table. As if I was a wolf among an unfamiliar pack, I singled out the alpha. Slicker had braids that ran along the curve of his head; he hid them by putting on a hat. He was wearing sandals. His feet were the color of burnished bronze, refined in a furnace, and his voice was like a waterfall.

"Welcome to the party."

He sported a rough goatee that held moisture from the cups of co-deine that frequented his mouth. The smell of weed was in the air, and it was almost as strong as the smell in Old Boy's attic, even though we weren't in a grow house. The scene before me, as we stood in the presence of the guys, was so vivid I almost couldn't take it in. A large flat screen television played music videos, and the guys sitting on the couches in the living room eyed the beautiful women in these videos, even though they were surrounded by real, equally beautiful women. Slicker had one girl for each of his arms. One of them was passed out, and the other was smoking a cigarette and playfully blowing the ex-haust around Slicker's ear. It occurred to me that some people in the house were there for protection because the big, burly guests looked more like bouncers guarding a club. Some obscenity sung to a tune bombarded my ears; chemicals or the scent of some illegal substance tickled my nose. There were several to choose from. My eyes saw ev-erything that my mother would tell me to condemn, and my mouth hung wide open, ready to consume it all in one hasty gulp.

"You lettin' kids in just like that, Slicker?" someone asked.

All eyes were on Slicker, who didn't answer. One of Slicker's hands took the cigarette out of his mistress's mouth, and his other hand crept closer to the upper thigh of the other girl, the one who was uncon-scious. She wasn't bothered by the curiosity of Slicker's digits. She yawned with a smile on her face.

"That ain't no kid," Slicker said matter-of-factly. "That there's my man's Old Boy!"

The posse ate up Slicker's enthusiastic declaration of Old Boy as "his man's" and laughed.

"Who that with 'em though?" Slicker inquired at me.

"I'm, uh, Cedric," I introduced myself.

"Nigga, did he talk to you?" growled one of Slicker's posse members.

The guy was huge and covered in tattoos of every weapon known to mankind. I shook my head no.

"Who is he?" Slicker asked Old Boy.

"That's Cedric," Old Boy answered, needlessly pointing to me.

"You taking care of my weed, right?" Slicker asked sharply.

"Yessir!" Old Boy responded.

"Well then, what y'all want?" Slicker asked.

I felt the stares of a dozen people. Even the girl who blew smoke in Slicker's ears stopped her flirtatious antics to look at me. Her hair was styled in a bob that had been doused artistically in pink dye. She had gold hoop earrings that hung from petite earlobes and purple lipstick that made her seem as if she could seduce all living males. As Old Boy went over to Slicker and explained why we were there, I let my mind wander over this girl's body. She noticed when I stared. A batted eyelash told me that she was flattered, but eventually she resumed flirting with Slicker, who was listening intently to Old Boy's request on my behalf. When they finished talking, Old Boy thanked him. I followed him out of the house.

"What'd he say?" I asked, thinking he had denied me.

"He said to wait in the backyard," Old Boy instructed. "I'll catch up with you after it's over."

Before I could object, he was already walking up the street back to his house. Wanting to follow instruction, I headed to the backyard, which was desolate and bland in comparison with the constant party that was happening inside. There was an old grill that hadn't been used; it was turned over to its side on the yellowish grass. Besides that grill and my soul, the backyard was empty. With no place to sit, I sat down on the yellowish grass and waited for someone to come talk to me. I waited for what seemed like hours and was almost going to go inside and remind them in case they'd forgotten about me when Slicker along with some of his posse came out the back door. Slicker was shirtless now, outfitted only with a thin layer of sweat. He had a bottle of wine in his hands, which seemed to have only been open for a short time, because it was mostly still full. He held it with power as though it had been a bottle of water before he touched it. The big guy with the tattoos walked with him as well as a thinner, scraggly looking dude.

Before I knew what was happening, the big guy with the tattoos had pinned me to the ground. I squirmed and opened my mouth to yell at him, but as soon as I did, I felt the wine running down my throat. There was a slow, powerful burn as it made its way down to my center, and I gagged at the unfamiliarity that was the pungent tang of alcohol. The skinny guy held in one of his hands a small vial of black ink and in the other a sharpened paperclip. I opened my mouth again, and again I was served additional doses of the sedative. After that, I stopped opening my mouth and just watched.

The skinny guy held up the sharpened end of the paper clip and an ostensibly floating hand, which must have belonged to someone, lit a lighter underneath the glossy point so that it gained the red tint of heated metal. Then he dipped the tip in the vial of black ink and went to work on the elbow side of my upper forearm. He repeatedly stabbed that area of my skin inconsiderately but also with care as he worked away at what I could only assume was some sort of emblem.

The pain was near indescribable. It was like being bitten over and over again by a vindictive stray dog that you might have petted the wrong way, only the dog had a single tooth that pumped a hot, gooey black venom deep into your wailing pores. I passed out, my body apparently too weak to endure what they dealt. When I came to, I was greeted by the smell of ribs, and for a moment, I thought I had died and gone to heaven...but heaven wouldn't have had yellow grass. Slicker and his posse had decided to have a cookout to celebrate my initiation. At least that was what he told me when I asked him. I turned my forearm over and saw an N with a downward arrow underneath it and then an S underneath that arrow, all of this under the cover of my dried blood.

"North over South," Slicker explained to me.

It was indeed an emblem. It could've been that I had spent too much time with Witt, but I became angry at the fact that they found this a necessary part of being in a gang, that I had been violated with a permanent mark. Still I thought it would be worth it. I was a part of North Gang, and people in North Gang made money. My fellow gang members offered me some ribs, having made use of the old grill. I respectfully refused. I learned how to do their shakeup, said my good-byes, and headed home. In all honesty, I was scared and wanted to distance myself from them as quickly as possible. On my way home, I finished convincing myself that what I had done was a good thing.

"Money for Josiah…money for Josiah…money for Josiah."

I repeated this over and over again. He would make it in life; he had to make it. I would make sure of it. I walked with an irregular strut, partially due to the pain, but also because I felt an unwavering confidence for the first time in my life. It was seventy-five degrees warm that evening and still two years before I'd be able to call myself eighteen, five years before I'd be able to legally ingest what I had, more than one hundred and sixty years since I'd walked this way on my day of reckoning, but on that evening I felt *eighteen cool*.

Fighting my single-minded goal of getting back home, I stopped to look at a group of faces through the window on the front side of the house. It was some of Slicker's gang. They were laughing along with the pretty girls as if nothing had ever happened. They were laughing as if they hadn't just branded a boy. Whatever disgust I felt wasn't strong enough to undo the effects of my eighteen cool, but I did feel uneasy. I wanted to give him a piece of my mind, but I figured most people didn't get promoted by cussing out the boss. Besides, I couldn't put that money for Josiah in jeopardy.

I flipped it back and forth in my mind as I walked home. I had gone out and done the exact thing Witt had warned me about. I justified it by telling myself it was for the greater good, *his* greater good. The truth was the familial structure that supported him was structurally unsound. I arrived home just in time to see it collapse.

A suspicious car was parked in front of our house. It wasn't nice enough to belong to Witt. My mother was at work, and my dad had taken the day off because he wasn't feeling well—at least that was what he had told us. I was not expected to be back for a while, but with my new tattoo and gang status, I needed to go home to process it all. So many thoughts were going through my head; maybe that was the reason I didn't recognize whose car it was.

"No, baby, no one's gonna be home for a while. Come over. It'll be just the two of us. We can have all the fun we want."

When I walked up to the door, I found that it was already cracked open. There was absolute silence. The only sign that something wasn't right was a white feathery mess of a woman's coat that overpowered our coatrack. Naturally I didn't see it. I was removed from my trance when I tripped over something, but I resumed it again when I got up. What did I trip over? A pair of pink flats that had no place being on the welcome mat. I didn't notice them either.

"Hang your coat. Damn, why is it so big? Get it off you so I can touch you."

I kept walking. I came into the living room. Except for a slightly misplaced cushion, nothing was strange. I walked over to it and thumped the corner into the confines of where the backrest met with the abyss of missing remotes, spare change, and assorted lint. A scent was in the air—like bug spray trying to disguise itself as something less austere, sweet even, but not quite. Whatever it was, it had started from a central point and then, through the law of diffusion, wafted outward in all directions, laying claim to every wall, corner, and particle of air.

"Do you like my new perfume, Lucius? I bought it just for you! It's called Arôme de Petite Mort...fancy, ain't it?"

I was a bit hungry, so I made my way to the kitchen, missing multitudes of hints along the way, until I came to the fridge. I opened it. As usual, it wasn't exactly overflowing with food. I still remembered what had been in it that morning: two liters of apple juice, one tomato, two heads of lettuce, one thing of butter, two bags of bread, half a gallon of milk, and an unopened bottle of white wine. But when I looked, what I saw differed from what I had seen that morning: two liters of apple juice, one tomato, two heads of lettuce, one thing of butter, two bags of bread, half a gallon of milk, but no bottle of wine.

"I got something just for you too. Gus from the liquor store held it just for us. What? No, he don't know. I just told him it was for a special someone. Go get you a glass."

I drank the apple juice straight from the carton; it was cheap, but, boy, was it good. When I had taken down a lot more than I should've, I placed it back into the refrigerator. I was actually considering going out again when I heard a noise come from the hallway; something was in the bedrooms. All the bedroom doors were closed except for the one at the end at the hallway, the master bedroom. Usually that was the only one closed.

"I don't know, Lucius, in her own bed? It seems wrong. It is wrong. No, I know you put a lot of effort into finally getting us some alone time, it's just...I know, baby, I know...the wine does taste good."

I heard noises. I heard noises that I had never heard before. I heard noises that I could never unhear. Still refusing to believe that I was hearing what I was hearing, I walked forward. With every step, the noises became louder and louder. Rushed breaths. I kept walking. I hoped that when I got to that cracked open door and peeked in I would see nothing. I hoped it had all been a hallucination, most likely from my alcohol consumption. But when I peeked in, I saw them. They were in bed together, a sheet hovered over them in the shape of a hump, and their every movement caused the sheet to transmogrify. With every thrust, the sheet changed shape like the belly of a pregnant woman did when the baby kicked.

They didn't notice me, and they kept on going. He kissed her down her neck until his lips reached her breasts, and it was her breasts that muffled what he huffed next: "I love you." Those three words that I had only heard him say to my mother, Josiah, and me when I was younger. Those three words that bound our family together, that fanned the flames of hope that we had. He said those words to her.

They kissed some more, and I felt nauseous. I felt as if I was going to throw up my very life. I wanted to look away, but I couldn't. I wanted to walk away, but my feet were stuck as if they had been nailed to the floor. If I had to observe, I wanted to see some sort of tell, some sort of indication of repentance, or regret, or shame. The sheet fell a little, fainting into the grooves of his sweaty back, and in one swift motion, he grabbed two fistfuls of Lucille's bushy hair. He slowed to a stop like the coupling rods on a train nearing its station. He gasped as though he was in pain, and then, having achieved what he wanted and no longer distracted, he saw me.

"Every time it gets better and better—" Lucille stopped talking once she saw me. "Oh my God" was all she was able to say.

She slipped out from underneath my father and rolled over so that I could only see one shiny shoulder.

"Oh my God. Oh my God. Oh my God," she said over and over again as she cried.

My father couldn't look away from me, and I couldn't look away from him. He must've seen the judgment in my eyes. His mouth hung wide open. He was still breathing hard. His eyes slowly fell to the ground, and he shook his head. He made noises with his mouth that almost sounded like words as he tried to build an explanation, but he had forgotten the dynamics, I guess. His words dropped from his mouth like rocks falling into a pale pond, each ripple a syllable searching to make sense of itself. He tried to attach meaning to them, to tell me his guilt, to make words that were paramount, carefully constructed, the kind of words that could erase time, words that might move me to forgive him. But his words held no weight, and yet they sank, word after word, down to the bottom. The man I saw before me was bare and bargaining for a forgiveness that I could not give. That man was stunned by his own sin, and I had no pity for him. So I backed out of the room and closed the door on the man I once called my father.

XX

He left shortly after the incident. He'd seen it in the way that I had looked at him that he was dead to me, so for the second time I lost a father. Even my first father had only taken one wife when he was expected to take more. What was his excuse?

When someone was dead to you, you were just as well dead to them even if they didn't want you to be. A relationship was a two-way street, and I had put up an impenetrable blockade, so he left. He didn't even take most of his belongings.

Lucille got dressed up, still crying, trying to regain her decency with each article of clothing. My father did the same. When he was fully dressed, he pulled out his suitcase, and when the suitcase was full, he left. He didn't even drive. He just walked out hanging his head as though he'd just been fired from his job, which he was inevitably because he didn't show up for it. He just walked away and never came back, and I was all right with that. My mother, on the other hand, was not. I told Josiah, and he seemed to understand the situation perfectly, but I could not bring myself to tell my mother.

"He left" was all I could say.

She pretended not to know *why* he left, just as I had for so long. But when she called Lucille to worry, Lucille never picked up. When she filed a missing person report and handed out flyers around the neighborhood, Lucille kept her doors locked. Lucille avoided us as though we were matching magnets. So it went on like that, my mother having two and two in her mind but refusing to put them together, until her refusal to accept the unacceptable started to take its toll on her. She never smiled anymore after my father left. She never laughed either. All she did was work and drink to take the pain away, and so the dead queen died again.

Simpler Times...

"Cedric, come on, we have a couple errands to run!" my dad called. His voice instantly drew my attention away from chatting with the other children. I ran to him. He picked me up, walked around to the passenger side of the car, and put me in the front passenger seat of the car. It was a rare (and illegal) thing for me to sit in the front. It had been the end of another hard day in Mrs. Keaney's kindergarten class. My day had been filled with the toil of trying to teach little Joshua James how to write eights in one motion instead of two circles on top of each other. I told this to my dad, and he did a good job of feigning interest in between beeping at sluggish traffic.

My father could've been a great actor. He was good at making the people he loved feel safe and important as if nothing else or no one else in the world mattered to him. He was good at making his friends feel as though they had no problems, and he was good at making things seem peaceful even when I knew they weren't. He had this old-timey sentimentality to him. He was the kind of man who could spend years building a house, knowing that it would be knocked down by an impending tornado, and still leave the rubble with a grin on his face. He was also "powerful" in every sense of the word as well as uncannily clever; he was kingly. All of these things—and for some reason, he couldn't hold a marriage together.

I knew he was treating me to the front seat to make up for something, but I didn't know what yet. In the side mirror of the car, I could still see the outline of my school in the distance. It had been a foggy morning, and the wind, having failed to clean the air, made it so it was a foggy afternoon as well. I saw through his great acting enough to see the faint signs of distraught on his face, hiding just underneath his plastered-on expression.

A few months earlier, my father had purchased a small two-bedroom apartment in Martinville, a small sister town to ours. Before that we had lived in public housing in the part of Widower's Grove where the widowers were made. Through nothing but arguments overheard, I collected bits of information.

The first thing I knew about it was that it was an argument starter. Apparently the apartment was expensive considering we were just making enough not to need government housing, and it didn't allow us to, as my mother put it, "live comfortably," although my father would argue that living comfortably in the apartment wouldn't include wedging chairs under our doorknobs in fear that some invader would break our locks. It wouldn't include not being able to open the windows in fear of a rogue bullet. Living in the apartment would not include buying big blankets for heat in the winters and resorting to partial nudity to stay cool in the summers. The second thing I knew about the apartment was that for some reason me and my mother could not go live there immediately. All I knew about this was that every few days something would disappear from our home in the projects and that my father was gone a lot. I was young, and I didn't understand the concept of moving meaning manually relocating your belongings. I thought that every house and apartment came with furniture already in it. The third thing

I knew was that my mom suspected him of cheating, but this fact, even back then, I suppressed. The fourth thing that I would come to know was that we were headed to the apartment.

It took me a while. I knew something was different when we passed the main road that took us to our neighborhood and continued toward the town's welcome sign. An immense excitement started to fill me. I had never actually been to the apartment before. What I did know of it in terms of how it looked came from little snippets that I'd seen from real-estate pamphlets with our selection firmly circled in red. For a while we drove past some woods. My eyes darted back and forth from the window to the corner of my dad's eye, and I rested my hand right on the door handle as an army of dark-brown spindly trees zipped past me in a blurry gothic mess. I was anticipating our new home to come into view so that I could immediately hop out. I was glad that he was taking me with him.

It was dark when we got there. To my amazement, he drove right up to it, an astounding feat considering it was surrounded by buildings that looked exactly like it. Boxy beige-colored apartments swarmed every lot in sight. We got out of the car, and he led the way to our new paradise. As soon as you entered the building, you were greeted by a row of mailboxes. To me the impressive thing was that they were actual sized mailboxes and that they lined the wall in a continuous row so that you couldn't tell where one stopped and another started. To any child who hadn't already been inside the building, the sight would merit a few seconds of admiration, but my father just kept walking. He walked up the steps but made sure to put weight only on certain places. I followed his lead, and when I asked him about it, he told me that some of the steps creaked and that he liked to keep our new pad dead silent. I nodded in confused, childish understanding. After passing multiple identical doors with similar numbers, he stopped at one that read "0023." He then looked down the hall, first to the left and then to the right, to make sure nobody was watching. Next to this door was a poster that had a picture of a cruise ship on it. He quickly peeled the poster from the bottom right corner to reveal a hole in the wall.

"Guess it's not so perfect after all," I said smugly.

My dad smiled. "See, that's where you're wrong, little man."

He reached his hand into the hole, pulled out a key, then shoved the key into the lock, and turned. I was severely disappointed by it. It wasn't all that bad, just a far cry away from what I had expected. I didn't understand what he liked so much about the apartment. Besides furniture, a welcome mat, and framed quotes of famous people on the wall, as well as a few other amenities, it had little to show. The walls were beige just like the outside of the building, and the view outside the window was terrible, as it showed the beige backside of another apartment building.

But as I got comfortable, I could see why my father appreciated it. Maybe liking this place was genetic; our family line wasn't one of wonted glamour. Mainly there were three reasons to like it: it was spacious, clean, and quiet.

"So you come here to work on work stuff while we're moving in?" I asked.

"Well, yes, and other things, like reading the newspaper or reading a book or watching TV or exercising or whatever I feel like doing that day. I've wanted this apartment way before we decided to move, and the best thing about it is that it can be whatever we need it to be," he said.

"But it's a little boring, and what about the view?"

My dad walked over to the window and pulled up two blinds to reveal a fantastically dull light-brown hue.

"I like it boring," he said. "I can't get any work done on anything if I got a view of a great big city or train station or something. Boring is good in moderation, and, well, this apartment is perfectly boring."

All of a sudden, it dawned on me that my father might be wise, which had never dawned on me before. He hadn't gone to college or even finished high school, but he managed to work his way up in a series of odd jobs that eventually led to him working as a carpenter. He drew up floor plans on the side for construction.

"How did you get so smart?" I asked.

My father looked at me with satisfaction, as though he had waited for me to ask him that his whole life.

He cocked his head back, grinned a little wider, and said, "My father, of course. I don't think I've ever told you about your grandfather. Do you want to know about your old man's old man?"

He walked to a small patch of carpet overlooking the tile kitchen. On this little length of carpet was what you could consider the closest thing to a dining room that the apartment had. There was a large glass table with a single can of beer on it. It might've looked classy if it wasn't for the wood frame that was old and discolored and rotting a bit at the edges. My father sat down on a wooden chair and pulled out another one for me. I took a seat.

"Well, there isn't a lot to say about your old grandad. He was a good guy. He met my mother when he was in high school, and it turns out, they were both headed to the same small town to start their adult lives." My dad chuckled.

"It wasn't long after they'd found jobs and rented out a tiny little hut of a house that they had me."

"What was Grandpa's name?" I asked.

My dad's eyebrows rose in surprise. "Jesus, I almost thought I forgot. Howie. His name was Howie Burgan. Turns out it's tradition to name the firstborn Howie."

This intrigued me.

"What if it's a girl?" I asked.

"Then you name her whatever you want, I guess. I wasn't gonna give that name to any of my boys though because it's based off a lie. But I know why it's a tradition. You see, ask any of the black Burgans up north in Mississauga, and they'll tell you that we all got the wrong last name. Yep, the wrong last name, and it's all Harriet Burgan's fault."

I puckered my lips, contemplating the info as my father continued.

"Harriet Burgan was a fine woman who worked at a small café in Mississauga back in the thirties. Legend has it that she was so good she could remember your exact order from a whole year ago. Anyway she was good at her job, but she wasn't gonna be nobody important, that is, not until one day when this gentleman strolls into the café. Well, he's young and smart, and she ain't never think about anything but work, but that day she couldn't take her eyes off this gentleman. Short story short, she ends up pregnant, and she don't even get the guy's name! That would've been the end of that, but some lady who had seen the man in the café said she recognized him as a small-time poet, Langston Hughes."

I didn't know who Langston Hughes was at the time, but from the way my father said his name, I knew he was important. I listened on.

"So she has a son, names him Howie Hughes Burgan, and ever since then people in our family been naming their kids Howie. Like I said, it's all a lie. There ain't no way Langston Hughes could've been in Canada at that time," my father explained.

"Why not?" I asked.

"Oh, I don't know why not *exactly*. I just know enough about Langston Hughes to know that he wouldn't be in no Canada in the thirties and that the man never had any kids. I thought about naming you Howie anyway, but your mom wasn't having it. My dad ain't believe in that bull, and it's supposed to go to your firstborn not second, so I named you Cedric."

He took a sip of beer. I never knew about this family tradition. What else didn't I know? I didn't like not knowing, and maybe learning more about my roots could help me recognize my leaves—my strengths and weaknesses, what made me tick, and what made me stop. Maybe I could learn what ancestral hand was writing my letter eights.

"Tell me more, Daddy," I urged.

"It's getting late, Cedric. The couch unfolds into a bed. I can sleep there, and you can sleep in the bedroom," he said, trying to end the conversation, but I wasn't having it.

"No! Tell me more about Grandpa!" I begged.

My dad was in the middle of getting up from his seat, but he paused, looked at me, and then sat back down.

"Well, what do you want to know, kid?" he asked.

I thought for a moment. Usually when my dad said he was done with something, he stuck to it and didn't change his mind, but I guessed my begging made him feel guilty. Only seconds passed, but the silence made it feel like an eternity. Just when it looked as though my father's patience had run dry and his face was starting to contort from anxiousness...

"How did he die?" I finally said, not being able to think of anything else to ask.

Crickets. Literal crickets. Night had stalked us, and its presence was revealed by the chorus of crickets that started chirping along. One by one each of them joined in, completely spontaneous and yet right on cue.

"Cedric, are you sure you want to talk about that?" my dad asked.

"Yes," I answered.

My dad took one big gulp of beer and then sighed as he recalled.

"I guess if it hadn't been *my* pops, I would've found the way he died kind of interesting instead of just sad. The way your grandpa died was kind of ridiculously unexpected. He cleaned the windows of big corporate skyscrapers for a living, so the risk factor was already there. He died a few years after I left home. It was terrible. I still remember when my mom got the call saying that a gang shooting had broken out while he was walking to work. There had been three girls standing right in the crosshairs between these gangbangers, and your grandad—being the man he was—had covered those three girls with his body. They survived, but your grandad was shot seven times, and he died. I couldn't believe it. All those years, dozens of stories up, and he never got hurt, but just one shootout was all it took. I don't think he was collateral damage though. I think they might've been targeting him for something. He died a hero, but I don't know...he didn't seem right in the days before it happened, you know? He didn't seem like himself. He always was getting into trouble, but that had been when he was younger...before my time. But those days before it happened, you'd look into his eyes sometimes and see that there wasn't much looking back at you, and that was if he did decide to look back at you. He was a good man, but I think he might've messed with the wrong people. I think he lost himself. Crazy how one moment you have a father that you think you know and then the next the man you see is almost a stranger. All right, now off to bed, Ced, I mean it. I don't want you having nightmares. Gotta keep my boy rested up for kindergarten. I love you."

We didn't live in the apartment for long. Eventually we couldn't afford it, and we had to find a home right in the heart of the last place we wanted to be.

> Regretfully I must declare, that there is angst in the old man.
> He loves his other half halfheartedly, oh what a sad sham.
> Medusa meddles meticulously; hell lies within her soft hands.
> Fire froths from her fingertips; don't burn the mamma—you can't.

Young child, young child, that is not thee,
His life spirals down uncontrollably,
Cries for help, a soliloquy.
Lord save his troubled soul.

Regretfully I must declare, that there is angst in the young man.

XXI

Old Boy had known what they were going to do to me. When I met up with him at school, he rolled up one of his sleeves without me saying anything and showed me an identical tattoo.

"North over South," I said.

He laughed nervously.

"Sorry about leaving you like that," he apologized. "I didn't want to be there for the initiation."

"That's all right," I said.

"You okay, Cedric? You look like you just seen a ghost."

"Yeah, I'm fine," I lied. I had been a little angry at him, but I was the one who had decided to join; he hadn't forced my hand in anything. "I mean the worst of it is over."

Old Boy's grin told me I was wrong.

"What?" I asked.

He stayed quiet.

"What?" I asked again, louder.

"You got to complete a job for him," he fessed up.

I didn't understand what he meant. "What kind of job?"

"Whenever Slicker and them get a new recruit, they make them complete a job so they know that you can handle things that need to get done. They leave you alone after it's done mostly. They just need to make sure you can handle the lifestyle, is all," Old Boy explained.

I felt a bit of heat rush to my face.

"Sometimes they pay pretty good though," he added, trying to defuse me before I went off.

"Like enough to bail Jo out?"

"I don't know about that, Cedric, but enough to knock how much you'll need down by a few levels."

"What did they make you do?" I asked out of curiosity.

"Well, that's a part of the problem for me. I haven't done a job yet. Neither has Xavier."

"Since when did Xavier join?" I asked.

"He joined them some time ago, but he hasn't done a job either, so he's not really a part of them," Old Boy explained. "Newbies are supposed to head over to this dude they call El Antonio to get some gang work."

With my initiation only partially complete and Old Boy's and Xavier's long overdue, we decided to head over to El Antonio the moment we got the chance, all three of us.

El Antonio's "headquarters" were in a generic white van. We had almost passed it when we heard a voice whisper Xavier's name. Two back doors opened, and we quickly got inside. El Antonio had wavy dark hair that formed a quiff that spilled over his forehead. He had dark stubble just above his upper lip, a large beak-like nose, and a mole on his left cheek. He had a marginal space in between his top two front teeth; the only way you could notice was by a bright red straw that filled the gap. For some reason, he chewed on this straw constantly as though he was in an old Western or something. Maybe he thought it made him look tough, which admittedly it kind of did. He had on a white tank top that exposed his large muscles. He had two tattoos. On his right arm, one read "El," and on his left, another read "Antonio." It was kind of stupid. I could think of no reason why he needed to be reminded of his own name twenty-four seven. He spoke with a heavy Spanish accent, but something told me he tried to sound more Spanish than he actually was.

"I usually don't allow new faces in my headquarters, but if Xavier says you're cool, then I'll let you hombres slide," he said as he chewed loudly on the straw.

The only things inside the van were posters that covered up the walls, mostly of Mexico (although I could've sworn it was Australia), a comically small stool, on which El Antonio sat, and an expensive-looking computer and keyboard sitting on a table backed up against the wall.

"What seems to be the problem? Do you want me to background check some bitches for you?" El Antonio asked Xavier.

Xavier laughed nervously. "Nah, nah, it ain't that."

El Antonio did some typing on his keyboard and gave Xavier a worried look. "Are you sure? The last girl you passed on background checking, remember that? I could do a complimentary check."

Xavier's *eighteen cool* momentarily evaporated. "No, El Antonio. Slicker sent us. He says we need to do a job to get into the gang. Mostly we need one for the newest member," Xavier explained, pointing at me.

"I need something that'll get me five thousand dollars," I said.

"And I need a beautiful senorita who only cooks and makes love and doesn't ask any questions." He laughed.

"You don't wanna piss off Slicker. You of all people should know that, man. He don't play," Xavier reminded him.

El Antonio adjusted his red straw with his fingers. "There're hardly any jobs right now, amigo…definitely none that'll net you that cash," he said flatly with a shrug.

"Why do you have pictures of Australia on your van when you said you were from Mexico?" I asked. The curiosity had gotten the best of me.

"What are you talking about? Those are genuine pictures from Mexico." El Antonio pointed at his posters as if he was accusing them of something.

"But I really don't think Mexico has those cactus species," I said.

Xavier glared at me, telling me to shut up.

El Antonio was giving me a death stare too. "The fuck wrong with you, nigga? If I say it's Mexico, then it's Mexico! I don't care if there's a fucking kangaroo with a koala in its pouch, if Antonio says Mexico, then it's Mexico. The fuck is wrong with your friend?"

He shifted his gaze to Old Boy, sizing him up as well.

"*Los hijos entrometidos,*" Old Boy said with a nervous smile. El Antonio looked as though he was going to break Old Boy's jaw. "This one's all right," he said finally.

He laughed to our relief.

"Okay. I'll help y'all out. There are no jobs, no small ones—delivering alcohol, organized vandalism, roughing people up, things of that nature…but there was a robbery a few days ago. One of my friends got a very expensive gold chain stolen from him," he said.

"You want us to get it back to him?" I asked.

"No, I want you to get it back to me. Forget that bitch-ass *culero*; he owes me money anyway. The chain's branded, and it isn't out yet. It's worth about fifty grand. I can pay you two grand if you get it to me, and of course I'll report to Slicker and tell him you all did well. Also, I'll keep him out of the loop so he doesn't come asking for his share," El Antonio offered.

"That's a start on the bail money, but I'm not one to steal. It is theft we're talking about," I said.

"And breaking and entering, home invasion, and assault and battery...well, assault and battery only if you're feeling adventurous," El Antonio chimed in. "Two grand. Take it or leave it."

"We'll take it!" Old Boy accepted.

Xavier and I looked at him.

"*Bueno!*" El Antonio said as he handed me a packet of paper.

On the top left-hand corner was a small picture that showed a Latino man who looked to be in his midtwenties with a goatee. On the top right corner was his name.

"Quatro?" I said aloud.

"I assume he has a real name, but this guy has at least one cat trying to murk him at any given time, so that's what he goes by...probably to protect whatever family he's got left," El Antonio explained. "He lives in a big house at the top of a hill in the suburb of Colonial Grove. The address should be in them papers. The times that he leaves his house are also in there somewhere. Be careful. He's a bad guy. He's dangerous. He deals drugs," El Antonio warned.

"And you don't deal drugs?" I asked.

"That's beside the point. This guy sells the hard stuff. If I was getting the chain back, I wouldn't want to run into him, but I'm sure he'd be very understanding about the trespassing. He's a very *Mi casa es su casa* kind of guy."

"Old Boy, what were you thinking accepting something like that?" I scolded as I slammed the door to his house behind me.

"He gave you an opportunity, and I took it, or do you not want Jo to get to mix for B&B records?" Old Boy defended.

"Fine, then why don't *you* go to Quatro's house and steal back that gold chain?" I said.

"You got me fucked up. I don't know why you copping an attitude. I'm only trying to help you and your blood out." Old Boy shook his head. "Look, if we really can't do this, then we'll just go back to El Antonio and tell him we can't do it, simple as that."

"No, it's not as simple as that," Xavier started as he dove face-first into the couch. He loudly moaned into the cushion before lifting his face up again. "Nigga, we can't just take it back. El Antonio has a very strict no-return policy on these little job opportunities. The last guy who wouldn't accept a job after he had already taken it didn't end up very well." Xavier's face looked grim.

"Where did he end up exactly?" I asked.

"Look, El Antonio isn't a bad guy at heart, but he knows a lot of really bad, really dangerous people. I heard one of those people drowned the guy or shot him...either way they never found his body. We can't just bitch out. Y'all don't get it. This is gang shit, and if El Antonio don't send no goons after us, then Slicker's ass will, especially if he finds out we cut him out of a deal."

Basically, what I was hearing was that we would have to do it on the possible threat of murder. I was never one to go against the law, at least not this far against it, but I reminded myself that I had asked for it and it was my own fault.

"Where does he live?" I asked after a long silence.

"He lives on the highest house in Colonial Grove. I guess I know that suburb pretty well," Xavier answered.

"The papers say he's away from his house on Tuesdays and Thursdays basically for the whole day," Old Boy added.

Xavier got up from the couch as Old Boy sat down. I could hardly believe it, but we were seriously working out how we were going to pull this off.

"Fine, all right, we don't really have a choice, but we're going to need some things," Xavier said, pacing the living room.

"What things?" I asked.

"I've done this one time before, and we're not just going to strut up to his house in bathrobes and sandals. We're going to have to look the part and know what we're doing. That means masks, dark clothing, probably weapons too in case things get ugly." Xavier paced faster, trying to concentrate.

"What do you mean you've done this once before?" Old Boy asked.

"You do a lot of things in eighteen years" was all Xavier said.

He made a rough outline of a plan for us to follow. The more he talked, the more I listened and the more I started to believe that we could actually pull it off.

We're in Luck...

"So what exactly are we about to do?" Old Boy asked as if I hadn't already told him multiple times.

"We're here to get as much info on Quatro's house as possible," I answered again.

"And how do you suppose we gon' do that?" Old Boy asked.

"All we're going to do is look around his house," I answered.

"In a suburb?" Old Boy, as usual, looked confused.

He was right though; snooping in a small neighborhood would attract attention, but we needed to scope out our playing field. The bus ride to the Colonial Grove subdivision was long. A bus ride would have been no big deal if it wasn't for the fact that the bus's air conditioning broke down midride. It was unusually warm, and Colonial Grove was in the hills, which meant the bus had to drive slow.

"You so lucky," Xavier told me as he fanned himself with a bus-route pamphlet.

"Why is that? Is my seat cooler than yours? Because I'll tell you right now it isn't," I joked.

"No, because you have friends who would ride in this oven for the sake of your big bro."

Xavier laughed, increasing the speed of his fanning as beads of sweat ran down his face. I smiled and looked out the window. Houses four stories high started to line up. I understood the appeal of living up in the hills; it was quiet and secluded. It was away from everyone else, which gave it an exclusive feel.

"I would give my left nut to live in one of these houses."

Xavier was in awe of the houses. I glanced at him, but the only thing I could see was the back of his head pressed up against the bus window. I decided to do the same. The sweat plastered my face to the glass close enough so that any movement made a squeaky wiping noise. The houses were admirable. Stucco roofs topped yellow walls masquerading as gold under the sunlight. Picket fences circled the properties like a pearl necklace circled a woman's clavicle. Flowers and bushes decorated the lawns. It was obvious that they were routinely cared for, but I didn't think it was the actual owners of the house who did the work.

"Bourgeois as hell," Old Boy said under his breath.

It reminded me of what I wished our old apartment had been.

The bus came to a slow halt, and we got off. Quatro's house stuck out like a sore thumb. It was at the very top of a hill. On that hill were numerous houses, each one trying to be just as big, just as bold, just as grand as Quatro's place and all of them failing. The papers had told us a lot of things, but what it forgot to mention was the fact that a ten-foot-tall black steel fence with a security guard in a kiosk planted right beside the mailbox surrounded Quatro's house.

His audacity was impressive—bought the biggest house on the biggest hill in the most exclusive suburb. He was different from what I thought a big-time drug dealer would be, different from how we had to be if we were going to break into his home. He wasn't afraid of drawing attention, while we were terrified of it. He wore his drug money on his sleeve and then raised his hand so everyone else could see it. He had audacity, I could give him that, but not without taking that chain. We walked up to the house in silence, partially because given the weather, talking might've induced heat stroke and partially because it left us speechless. Any bigger and it would've been a mansion.

"Hello, sir?" Xavier called out as he walked toward the kiosk.

"What are you doing?" I asked.

"I'm gonna go talk to the security guard," Xavier answered.

"And tell him what? 'Hey, we would like to scout out this house for when we come back and break into it in two days'?"

Quatro didn't have any video cameras. I figured it was most likely to reduce any digital evidence of his or his friend's involvement in the lucrative drug business. I grabbed Xavier's arm to stop him, but he pulled away from me.

"Xavier!" I called after him in a whisper.

Xavier held his hand over his forehead to block out the sun and walked up to the kiosk. He put his face right up to the glass, stood there for a while, and then walked back.

"I hear the heat can make people sleepy," he said with a smile.

We walked around the perimeter of the house. Old Boy pointed out that the neighbors were less likely to snoop because even if they did see us, calling cops to Quatro's house would be the last thing they would want to do. However, this was only an assumption, so Xavier suggested we move fast. We'd already decided there was no way we were going to jump the front gate, so we paced around the fence to see if there were any low points. We looked for shorter fence posts, but despite the hilly landscape, the height stayed consistent. We looked for trees with branches hanging over the fence, but an old stump revealed to us that Quatro didn't tolerate any trees like that. We looked for gaps in the fence post, any slightly oversized spacing that we might be able to squeeze through, but like the height, it stayed consistent. We had almost completely circled the house when we heard a loud bark. I put my face up to the fence, and sure enough, past a private backyard tennis court, partially obscured by a plant, was a Rottweiler. It was large and bulky, and slobber oozed from its mouth. Old Boy and Xavier reeled back in fear that it might run up to us, but they couldn't see the long leash that bound it to a column that kept up the awning to the back of the house.

"It's tied down," I said.

"Are you sure? I don't mess with dogs," Old Boy said nervously. "Dogs have teeth."

"Nigga, humans got teeth," Xavier said.

"It's tied down," I assured.

The real question was, why? Why would anyone tie up a guard dog while they were not home?

"Why would anyone tie up a guard dog?" I asked.

"I don't know, but I told you I don't mess with no dogs," Old Boy replied.

"I wasn't asking you, Old Boy. Xavier?"

Xavier scratched his head and thought for a moment. "Not too many reasons, I guess. To keep it from attacking guests, but that's if the owner's at home. Maybe to keep it from escaping, you know, jumping over a fence or something like that."

There was no way the dog could jump over the fence. It was too heavy. Not that there were that many dogs in the world that could clear ten feet, regardless of size.

"It could be a digger," I announced just as Old Boy confirmed my hunch.

"Hey, y'all, get over here." He motioned for us to come.

Sure enough, about two and a half feet deep and four feet wide was a hole under the fence. Quatro had noticed and put a pile of decorative rocks on the other side of the hole, enough to keep out any unwanted animals maybe, but not enough to keep out a newborn gangbanger. The hole—that would be our way in.

XXII

It had been Xavier's idea to bring along brass knuckles just in case of a confrontation. I reminded him that Quatro had weapons too and that you didn't bring brass knuckles to a gunfight.

"Okay, looks like we're all set." I closed the door to Old Boy's house behind me.

We walked outside, hoping that none of the neighbors would run into us. There were very few ways to explain the suspicious outfits. Desperate to avoid another faulty bus, I had asked Xavier to find us a ride. Something discreet, not too flashy, but fast and nimble enough to get us out of a bad situation. I figured he wouldn't be able to get the perfect fit on such a short notice, but he had managed to borrow an old black car from a friend. It was no Batmobile, but it wasn't as if we needed one anyway. Xavier had been the first out the door. He quickly looked left, then right, and then motioned for us to get into the car.

"Shotgun," Old Boy smirked as he opened the passenger-side door.

Xavier would be driving, so I made my way to the back. The back of Old Boy's seat and the front of mine strangled my legs, so I shifted over to sit behind Xavier. He turned the key, and just like that we were off.

When we got to Quatro's house, everything was just as we had remembered it, except darker. Just as the papers had said, it was Tuesday, and not a single light was on in Quatro's house. It was around ten o'clock when we got there, and as soon as we did, we got to work on the hole under the fence—more specifically *I* got to work. Old Boy squeezing under the fence was out of the question—although the thought of it was hilarious. My shoulders weren't as broad as Xavier's, so I had been the one to wedge myself between the metal and dirt and pick away at the tacky rocks. I could barely see what I was doing as it was very dark. Old Boy was helping me out though. He squatted and shone his flashlight as best as he could so that I could pick which stone to pluck carefully. I plucked one. Then another. Then when my grasp found an oval-shaped one, the whole mass of it crumbled onto my face.

"Cedric?" said Old Boy.

I didn't respond. A rock had fallen into my mouth, thankfully not slipping down my throat. Everywhere I looked all I could see were rocks and fractured rays of light trying to shove past the rocks from Old Boy's flashlight. I felt a pair of hands grip my leg. My left ankle felt ten fingers, and shortly after my right ankle, another ten. The two of them pulled me out of there easily, although the rough exit was made rougher by the mass of rocks sliding across my face. I spit out the one that was in my mouth as soon as I could and gagged a little at the taste of earth and minerals.

Once he made certain that I wasn't dead, Old Boy joined Xavier in picking out the rocks under the fence. They had all fallen from their position as blockades and were easy enough to pick out from the hole. The sound of stone clashing against stone did make a few hairs stand on the guard dog, who was sleeping loudly—his snores could rival a grown man. When the hole had been cleared, I squirmed into it first, followed by Xavier. He had to contort himself a little to make it, but he did. By unanimous decision, Old Boy would stay out and keep watch. We would keep an eye out for his flashing flashlight if anything went wrong.

The tennis court in the backyard was an inconvenience. Our shoes made noise against it, quiet enough for humans but all too loud in the ear canals of the dog kind. Luckily, we reached the back porch of the house without waking it. It was in reach of us. The rope that bound it to the house was long enough. I could reach out and touch if I only took a few more steps. Xavier reached into his back pocket and pulled out two pills. He carefully walked over to the dog, knelt down, and pulled down its wet jowls. The dog moved a bit, which startled us both, but after he downed the pills, we felt relieved.

"Those the pills we give Granddad to put him to sleep," Xavier explained. "And they make his old ass stay asleep," he added.

We waited for a couple minutes for some sign that the pills had taken effect. The only potential sign we got was a loudening of the dog's snores, which wasn't much, but it was enough for us. Xavier started to get to work on the sliding door. He produced a long wire along with a thin metal stick. I looked back at Old Boy, who was trying to watch us in the dark. He didn't dare shine his flashlight. His belly was pressed up against the bars of the fence, and his eyes popped halfway out of his head, trying to get a look at our plan in execution.

Click. Slide. Just like that we were in.

Quatro's house was well decorated. As soon as Xavier flicked on the lights, I was astonished by the vases and the framed artwork and the big candles that seemed as if they could burn for lifetimes. There was so much to see, in fact, that our search for the pricey gold chain was made a hundred times more difficult. I told my eyes to look for things that were yellow and shiny, trying to tune them like optical metal detectors. We needed to be quick because Quatro would be back within the hour. We didn't find anything, only created a mess. Xavier went to go look upstairs while I searched the rest of the ground floor in addition to turning over things we had knocked down. I looked outside as often as I could while I foraged around for the chain. Old Boy seemed to be a little more relaxed. He peered at the side of the house to make sure that the coast was clear, and then he held his thumb up to my relief. But before I turned around, he tapped an imaginary watch on his wrist. After a few more runs on the ground floor, I went upstairs to see if Xavier had found anything.

"Nah," he said bluntly.

I double-checked every drawer, every nook and cranny, every cabinet, hoping that my fresh set of eyes would pick up something that he had missed. We walked downstairs, back to the ground level, defeated. It was on the first floor next to his pantry that I zeroed in on a door that I had assumed was a closet. I tried to open it, but it wouldn't budge. Xavier was getting noticeably frustrated; his face was shiny with sweat, and his eyes darted back and forth rapidly. It was a good thing that his eyes were crazed because it was he who saw the flickering of the flashlight outside.

"Cedric, we gotta go," he said all of a sudden.

I looked outside to find Old Boy frantically flashing his light.

"This door is locked," I said as I jiggled the knob furiously.

"That doesn't matter now. We're out of time!" Xavier said, motioning for us to get out. He was by the back door.

"This is the only door that's locked—none of his bedrooms, none of his bathrooms, none of his closets, just this one," I said.

We heard a car door slam in the driveway. Xavier looked as though he was about to have a heart attack, but he calmed himself down quickly. Before I knew what he was doing, he rushed toward the locked door and busted it open, shoulder first. He almost fell down a flight of stairs, but I grabbed him before he could make the descent. We both skipped as many steps as we could on our way down Quatro's basement. It was the man cave of a successful drug dealer, everything luxurious. A flat-screen television that took up most of a wall was rivaled only in grandness by the black leather furniture that could seat a family of giants comfortably. Shelves on the walls were taken fully by paraphernalia: pipes, white bags, needles, test tubes, bottles of prescription medication—which I guessed weren't being used to treat illnesses. It went on and on. In the middle of it all was a coffee table, and on that coffee table was the brightest, iciest chain I had ever seen. While I spent the precious seconds we had taking in the sights, Xavier wasted no time in snatching the chain before pulling me by my collar all the way back up the steps. I could hear a key entering a lock as we made our way out of the house. The dog woke up and looked at us funny while we were on the back porch. He growled and tried to get up on his feet, but he was too drowsy to do so. He fell back and just watched incapably as we made our way to the fence to take the escape route that the poor thing itself had dug. Our dark clothes hid us well. The only light that came from us was the light from the flashlight and the few rogue beams that bounced off the exorbitant gold. We were kings that night, and we had our chain.

El Antonio paid me the money as promised. Xavier and Old Boy insisted on not taking any of it, but I gave them five hundred dollars each. They deserved a lot more, but Josiah needed as much of the money intact as possible. El Antonio also gave a good report to Slicker, who was impressed that we had completed one of Antonio's more difficult jobs. I kept the money in a shoebox under my bed. I'd wait till I had the full amount, and then I would pay in full. If I paid it in increments, he would have more time to ask where I got it from and reject it once I told him.

Over the next couple of weeks, Old Boy, Xavier, and I did lots of similar work for El Antonio. Compared to breaking into Quatro's house, the work we did was much easier, but I tried to go for the more difficult jobs whenever I could because of the higher payoff. It was exhilarating.

Witt called me as usual to check up on me, but as time went on, I ignored him more and more. We were a merry band of thugs who broke things and violated laws and had fun doing it. We were like natural disasters. Old Boy was an earthquake, rumbling the ground underneath with every clumsy step; Xavier was a lightning storm, bright and powerful; and I felt like a hurricane. I thought I was so powerful and so prosperous with the money I was making, the dream I was saving, and the fun I was having, I would get Jo out in no time at all. We had a few close calls, but we always got away. Old Boy shook the universe until it was forced to root for us, Xavier struck down on any black cats who tried to rob us of our mojo, and I unrooted four-leaf clovers and threw them to the sky; our luck would never run out.

Luck Runs Out...

First there was a hard stab of fear, and then came the running, running so fast individual steps became unidentifiable. The night air cooled my insides, but my outsides were what needed cooling. The heavy jacket I was wearing didn't help much either. It stuck to me and became bothersome luggage. I wasn't the only one. Someone was only a few paces ahead of me. How could he have been so stupid? How could he ruin everything in one thoughtless act of violence? I wanted to yell at myself, to remind myself of everything I had to lose, but I was running too fast to talk, and so all that came out was carbon—strong and in between teeth. All that came in was air. Although it was all around me, it felt as though there wasn't enough of it; it felt as though there would never be enough. It had gotten really bad in the previous week. I thought it would get better. I thought that the masks were only makeshift vices at worst. Everyone had thought it would get better. I'd dropped my mask a while back, and now my airways burned. How could everyone be wrong?

I ran through a field that lay just behind some random backyard. The field was commercial property waiting to be bought. It was well kept but not well enough; the thorns that snagged my pants and shoes told me that. I approached a tall wooden fence that guarded the yard. The other person running in front of me hoisted himself up, straddled the pointed top of the fence, and then winced in pain as he swung himself over. I looked closely at him. I couldn't tell whether it was Old Boy or Xavier. I did the same. I could hear the faint sound of sirens. They were growing less faint; the hunt was on. I knew the authorities around our parts had been the most aggressive in the past, and the new circumstances didn't help—us running around trespassing, hurting, and breaking things. I started running so fast it seemed as though my feet didn't even touch the ground anymore. I didn't know where I was or where I was headed. All I could do was follow the shadowy figure in front of me as it cut through yards and streets.

The figure turned back to look at me. He pointed his finger in the opposite direction as he made a sharp turn to the right. He didn't want us to go in the same direction. I knew that it was in my best interest to navigate away from him because it doubled my chances of not getting caught—that was basic street knowledge. I ran adjacent to the figure, making sure to keep a good distance. I cut through another yard, running at my top speed; everything was a blur as things whipped past my vision, and I knew I couldn't keep it up much longer. Trees, bushes, fences, I couldn't tell when one thing ended and another began. Instead, the scenery just jumbled together in an unsteady collage of suburbia. The sirens that once echoed in the distance behind me were all of a sudden loud, making sure everything that was able to hear was aware of their presence. I couldn't run any quicker. I tried to escape their boisterousness. The sirens were a torture. They scolded me as if telling me that joining had been my worst mistake, a depressing

symphony of hindsight. The sound was so nerve racking that I almost
didn't notice the crisp sound of tire touching concrete.

I was headed toward a highway. If this had been anywhere else,
then a highway would have meant nothing, but folks were notoriously
hitchhiker-friendly along this route. This wasn't Widower's Grove. If
I could stop a car and sling some bullshit, explain how my older sister
was having her baby, explain how I'd gotten a flat tire and my car had
just been towed, then maybe I could disappear into the myriad of cars
that shared the road. I would be safe at least for a while. All that kept
me from the highway was a wire fence that separated the neighborhood
from the highway. I launched myself over it, making the most out of my
already tired legs. It was only when I thought I had cleared it that I fell
to the ground with a hard thud. The green residue of crushed wet grass
stained my cheek. I tried to crawl away, but something was holding
me by my feet. I looked back; the fabric of my jeans had loosened and
tangled with the wire of the fence. I breathed so rapidly that I expected
my airways to close from overuse. The sirens still tortured me, only
now they were stationary. I could hear them coming for me.

"We need to make an example!" I heard one of them yell.

I had to get out now, otherwise I'd be done for. I desperately tried
to untangle myself from the fence with all of my strength, but it seemed
that every time I pulled I would only become more and more entwined.
I needed to get out, and I needed to get out quick. A rustling bush
caught my attention. It could've been the feds coming to take me away.
The figure from before jogged out from the foliage, frantically heading
for the highway; it became clear that we both had the same idea.

"Help! Help me out!" I called.

The figure looked back at me. It was Xavier, and his face was as
tired as I felt. There was something in his eyes too; it wasn't pity for
me but shame for him. He looked at the shadows that cascaded off the
foliage from the headlights that were only a few feet away from him.

"Come out!" a voice called.

Xavier looked in the direction that the voice was coming from and then back at me as I lay helplessly on the ground. He had a blunt in his hand. He took a long huff, and it was at that point that I knew he wasn't going to help me. I knew we were not innocent. He and I, we tore through things like tornadoes in unprepared Texas towns. We destroyed whatever we touched and leached value from whatever we stole. We crossed boundaries. We triggered anxiety. We instigated tension, wronging those who did nothing wrong. We stimulated stigma. We enacted our own particular stereotype without error. We were two sable terrors. We shredded up our habitat. We were young, we were crazy, and we were careless. We threw caution to the wind. We thought that was the sad, abrasive dictum of the young black male. This might have been minor had we not thought that it was the *only* dictum, the only possible title for the stories of our blue lives. And our black bodies slept in the mold of those blue characters wedged in pages that could never be unwritten. I wondered what I would've done, if I would've risked myself, risked disappointing Witt and freeing Josiah. Xavier puffed out a body of smoke, and then he turned and ran, leaving me behind. And just like that, my fate was sealed.

"Did you find anyone, Boyd?" I heard a police officer call.

He was on top of me. His breath smelled like death and rotten things. When he smiled his devious smile at me, he revealed the brand of toothpaste he used—molasses, only the darkest most tar-like kind. He took a knife from his pocket and sliced the thread that held me captive. I tried to squirm away, but his bony hand gripped me with a strength that was beyond his thin frame, the same frame that left his police uniform baggy and flat in places where a burlier man might've filled it.

"Boyd! Did you find anyone?" a police officer called again.

"No! Sweep round back. I'll meet up with you!" Boyd lied. He waited until he could hear the other officer wander off.

"You know why I just lied to Dale?" he asked.

I shook my head no.

"So he wouldn't have to see me do this."

With that, he kneed me hard in my stomach. I fell perfectly flat against the ground immediately. I tried to wrap my arms around my midsection to keep from throwing up all of my insides.

"Dale's a good cop, but he's too easy on you niggers," Boyd said.

I looked up at him. I almost didn't believe he'd just said what he'd said. On his chest was a big badge that read Officer Boyd Barnaby.

"That's right. I'm not gonna lie. I'm gonna call you what you are: a good-for-nothin' coon!"

He grabbed my earlobe and gave it a hard twist, and then he drove me further into the ground. The entire left side of my head was on fire, and my ear throbbed with pain. The cars still whizzed by, unaware of what was happening.

"I know you and your lot were the ones that broke into that apartment back there. You know how many folks live there?" he asked.

I was still trying to regulate my breathing. He leaned in close so that I breathed in what he exhaled.

"Do you know how many white folks live back there?" he asked real slow and gentle.

"No, sir," I said weakly.

"More people than your black ass ought to be disturbing. Just like your good-for-nothin' brother," he spat. "Now here's what's gonna happen next," he said as he reached for his baton.

I fell backward and slowly crab-walked away. "No, sir, please," I begged.

"Hold on now." Officer Barnaby laughed. "I could beat the shit out of you and leave on the side of the highway to rot, or you could tell me who the other boys were, the ones who were running with you."

"I don't know who they were," I lied.

He swung his baton against my head. I could tell that he wasn't using anywhere near his full force, but the pain was intense.

"Don't you lie to me, boy! You think I don't know about your little gang? They've been giving me and all my fellow officers hell for too long. I got a Glock twenty-two just itching to be used," he threatened.

"I don't know anything," I said. Tears were running down my face, and everything I saw was through a lens of saltwater.

"You came at me. I tried to get you to stay back. You kept on coming for me. I thought you were gonna kill me, nigger boy as big as you, so I defended myself. How does that sound?" He held his flat stomach and laughed, and then he put his baton away and stroked his pistol suggestively.

"No, sir," I begged. "Please, no!"

He didn't listen. He held the handle of his pistol loosely in his hands with a wide grin. It was at that moment that I considered the fact that I might die at his hands, with no witness to my death, no acknowledgment of my suffering. I didn't know what I was saying at the time, probably something along the lines of what I had been saying—the words "no" and "please" in no particular order followed by an inaudible explanation of why I should be spared. As I looked up at Officer Barnaby, I tried to provoke some kind of empathy from him, but there was no use. We might as well have been two separate species: he, the chosen one by the creator of the stars, which blinked curiously at my predicament, and I, his animal for him to do whatever he pleased.

In that moment when I thought I was going to die, I couldn't turn to a god who had no reason to help me. The ancestors were probably shaking their heads too. I could only face the man who had the gun.

If he chose to shoot it, there would be no last-second change of heart, there would be no spectacular escape, there would be no guardian angel to soften the blow, and there would be no bolt of lightning erupting from the stars to strike him. The only thing there would be was a bullet in me wherever he decided to put it.

I guess that was the beauty of free will. You did as you pleased even when it made others suffer. Laws might punish you after the fact, judgment might come later in many forms, but you could always do as you pleased so long as you had the gun. Maybe I deserved it. I had violated property and broken things, and now having thought myself a king, the moisture from my weeping and the pain in my body made me feel exactly that, violated and broken.

XXIII

Roger Barnaby had just gotten home from a long day of work at the factory manufacturing car parts. The headlights of his car sent two beams into his garage. There was a lot to see: a lawnmower, some power tools hung sloppily on the wall, a workbench with spare nuts and bolts on top of it, and some papers. As he sat in his car, he saw what his life had become over the years. He hadn't achieved what he had set out to accomplish. He might've if Lucy hadn't gotten pregnant.

"Roger, you went and got 'er knocked up, so you know what you gotta do. We ain't like them coons—we don't run off." That was what his father had told him.

It was unnecessary. Roger had no intention of leaving. He wasn't going to leave the burden of a baby on his high-school sweetheart, and he certainly was not going to lower himself to the standards of coons— that was out of the question. He stayed with Lucy. When she was red as an apple and the dome of a head had been peeking out of her, he was there, stoic and patient. When he had to cancel his dream of going to trade school so that he could look for a job and provide for his family, he was there. When the baby cried, when little Boyd became a faulty alarm clock, night after night, he was there. The fact that he was there gave him integrity, but the longer he stayed, the further away his dreams got in the assembly line of life. And all he asked in return was that Boyd keep his damned bicycle put up so that he could pull into the garage when he got home from work, and the stupid boy couldn't even do that. Roger got out of his car. Lots of people were in the house, which made sense at the time. The windows were open, and Roger could hear people talking and laughing. He slammed his door loudly.

"Oh, hey, honey!" Lucy greeted through a cyclone window screen. "How was work, babe?" she asked eagerly.

"Shitty," Roger replied.

Lucy's bright face, which reflected the festivities, suddenly went dark.

"Get Boyd out here!" Roger ordered.

Lucy pursed her lips and looked down as if she had done something wrong. She turned around and went to go fetch her son.

"Hurry up, woman!" Roger yelled.

She picked up her pace. The car was still running, and he was getting cold. He reached into his back pocket and pulled out a pack of cigs. He reached into his front pocket, careful to avoid touching his hanging beer belly—it only existed if he touched it. He pulled out a lighter and lit one up. He took a long drag on it, and he felt his insides warm. He tried to relax. He exhaled, and smoke slithered out of his mouth. He coughed, or he might've coughed—he couldn't tell. If he did, then it was drowned out by the sounds of cars speeding on the nearby highway, people enjoying themselves in his home, and the steadfast rumble of his old engine. Finally the boy emerged; a bob of blond hair bounced by the window. He opened the door, then the screen door, and then descended down the porch steps.

"Hi, Daddy—" Boyd said before his father gave him a hard slap across the face.

"Don't you 'hi, Daddy' me!" Roger barked.

He pulled up his brown belt angrily, jiggling his beer belly. Boyd's dirty-blond hair went from being in a layback mop to being swept to the side as a result of the strike. Four out of five of his father's fingerprints appeared in red on his white cheek. His eyes filled with tears as he tried to figure out what he had done.

"Don't you cry yet! What the hell did I tell you about putting up your bike?"

Boyd's eyes darted back and forth, and suddenly he remembered. "Sorry, Daddy," he said as he raced into the garage.

Roger sucked harder on his cigarette as the nicotine set in. He walked into the garage to find his son struggling to lift the bike. They hadn't been able to afford a new bike for their son, so they had bought one secondhand, and it was a bit large. Boyd eventually got the bike to stand, and he wheeled it out of the way. He was on his way out of the garage when his father said his name. He stopped walking, but he didn't turn around.

"You know what happens when you forget to put your bike up," Roger said.

"Please, Daddy," Boyd pleaded, but he knew it was already too late.

"Don't 'please' me. You should've thought about that before you left your bike in the middle of the garage," Roger said.

Boyd looked down. He turned around and walked to his father.

"You can choose which arm it is," Roger offered.

Boyd sniffled, thought about it, and opted for his left forearm. He rolled up his sleeve and held it out. Four semifaded dark circles were on his left forearm; it'd been a while since he had forgotten. Roger grabbed his son's forearm and took one last draw on the cigarette before lowering the end down to the skin. Boyd squealed, but he tried not to cry. The tiny spark of fire died down to the trademark sizzle, and a familiar smell of burning flesh filled the air, like bacon but more rotten. Roger gave the cigarette a few hard twists before tossing it on the lawn.

"Now go inside and have some turkey," Roger said, patting Boyd's head.

Boyd wiped his tears and headed for the porch.

"Oh, and son"—Boyd turned around to see what else his father wanted—"roll up your sleeve."

Boyd nodded, rolled up his sleeve, and went inside.

Inside people were a bit cheerier. Thanksgiving was being held at Roger's house, and most of the Barnabys' friends and family had shown up. The house wasn't very large, so there wasn't much space, but the people didn't seem to mind. All the men had forced their wives to cook for the occasion, and the result was a spectacular assortment of dishes: a bowl of edamame drizzled with soy sauce, collard greens with bits of pork, a golden potato gratin, squash casserole, plates of parsnips and grits, corn pudding, buttered rolls, lasagna outfitted with slices of pecan, turnip stew with a side of sautéed greens—the list went on and on, and every dish was a puzzle piece to the picture of ambrosia. The smell of it was so pungent that with one whiff you could taste a bite of every dish on the table. It was sweeter than any perfume.

Even during a social feast, everyone was split up into factions; the men took up most of the living room, and they all looked identical in the sense that they each had a beer in one hand, a plate stocked full of food in the other, and in each of their plates the centerpiece was a chunk of turkey. They all reacted the same when the quarterback went out wide and slipped behind the opposition's defense for a cool six points, and they all reacted the same way when the referee had given a six-yard penalty on the next possession for what they all agreed was "for no good reason at all."

"That's bull!"

And then as if none of them could hear each other and know that the phrase had already been said, they repeated it in slight variations.

"That's complete bull!"

"Total bull!"

"Yeah, that's so bull!"

They did this until someone would say something new.

"That ref is blind!"

Then that would be followed by "Yeah! Fire the ref!" and "That ref is an idiot."

The complaining would continue until their team scored.

In the kitchen, the women were in charge of cleaning. They shared in the work. Some scraped the leftovers in the trash, a few helped out with washing, and others provided the workforce with juicy gossip about everyone except the people who were there. They talked about whose kid was dating who, if Susan Manson had found a new husband yet, how far along Rachel from down the street was with her baby, who was making a killing from cosmetics and who wasn't, and whose kid had just done what for the first time or said the cutest thing you ever heard. They talked about hairstyles and baking and being mothers, and, in quieter voices, they talked about their husbands. The children were the last faction and the smallest. Most of the parents had invested in babysitters for the night, but there were still a good few at the party. They stayed in Boyd's room.

"There you are! What took you so long, Boyd?" asked the comedian of the bunch, Joey Horner.

Boyd bit his lip. "Nothing, I went to go get some seconds. I was really hungry," he said unconvincingly.

"You all right, Boyd?" asked orange-haired Trace Spitzer.

"Yeah, I'm all right," Boyd answered, trying his best to keep his voice from cracking.

Dennis Owen was sprawled out on Boyd's bed. He hadn't even noticed his friend return. His fingers tapped away at a handheld gaming device. He was at war with something on the screen. Boyd fell onto his bed like a falling tree landing face-first.

"Don't mess up my game, Boyd," Dennis protested. He grabbed a pillow and playfully whacked it on Boyd's head.

Boyd laughed.

Trace and Joey were talking about the latest wrestling match, specifically whether Tyler the Torturer's special move was better than Bob the Barbarian's.

"Bob can't move like Tyler can!" Trace said.

"He doesn't need to. He's a brick wall!" Joey rebutted.

"His special move is just hitting really hard, and the only reason Tyler lost last night's match was because Bob just absorbs punches!" Trace countered.

"Exactly, and if Bob's body was as thick as your skull, he might still be undefeated!"

Joey's comment resulted in a little laughter from everyone in the room, including Trace.

An awful digital sound erupted from Dennis's game system.

"That level's really got ya, hasn't it?" Boyd said, raising his head from his bed.

Dennis sighed. He tossed the thing near the foot of the bed and sat upright. "Enough about wrestlers. Let's talk about the really important stuff," he said.

"What?" the other three boys asked in unison.

"Girls," Dennis answered.

"Gross," Trace complained.

"Oh, shut up, Trace. I've seen you talking to Becky Henderson, and you weren't worried about cooties then," Joey said.

Trace's face warmed to a color closer to his hair.

"Well, now we know who Trace's crush is. I'll go next," Dennis volunteered.

There was a dramatic pause, and the other boys leaned in, not wanting to miss Dennis's misses.

"Cindy Foreman," he finally said.

"Cindy Foreman?" Joey laughed.

"What's wrong with Cindy Foreman?" Dennis asked.

"Goodness, what isn't wrong with Cindy Foreman? She cries about everything for one," Joey pointed out.

"She's just sensitive. She's a girl. Ain't nothing wrong with that," Dennis defended.

"Nuh-uh, I know the real reason you like her," Joey said with a foxy smile.

"There's something only I know," he said with nothing but a wink in Dennis's direction.

"What?" Dennis asked, searching Joey's eyes for the answer.

"Well, gentlemen," Joey started, "Cindy Foreman has boobs."

This piece of information caused the other boys' mouths to drop open into letter *o*'s. Dennis's mouth retracted into a sideways *I*.

"That…that is not the reason why I like her!" Dennis stuttered nervously.

"Is too!" said Joey, his grin growing wider.

"Well, it's not the only reason," Dennis replied. "She's pretty too," he added in a defeated whisper.

"All right, onto me then," Joey said, clasping his hands into prayer. He rubbed them together and hummed indecisively as he flipped through every prospect. Then he knew.

"I like Lori Larson," he announced.

"And you tried to get on my case for liking a girl with boobs when you did the same thing," Dennis accused.

"But there's a difference," Joey said, raising up his finger. "I'll actually admit it. I like her just for her boobs."

With three out of four of their loves professed, they all turned to Boyd, who had been listening but was not fully engaged in the conversation.

"Well?" asked Trace.

The boys were all sitting on the floor now in a circle.

"I, uh, don't know," Boyd said.

Joey rolled his eyes. "Yeah, you do. You're just too chicken to tell us," he charged.

"Hey, c'mon, Boyd. Everyone else spilled the beans," Dennis chimed.

Trace gave Boyd a hard, disapproving shove that sent him toppling over, but like a roly-poly toy, Boyd naturally straightened himself. All eyes were on him, and he knew that the rest of his night would not go smoothly unless he told them what they wanted to hear.

"Clementine Thatch," he murmured inaudibly.

"What? We can't hear you," Joey said, leaning in.

"Clementine Thatch," Boyd repeated, this time more firmly. "I like Clementine Thatch."

The other boys were taken aback.

"Clementine Thatch?" Dennis repeated. His brows lowered, and his nose and brows made a snarl as if he had just smelled something repulsive.

"The black girl?" said Joey worriedly.

"There's no one else named Clementine Thatch in our grade," Boyd replied.

His friends' awkwardness at his pick had caused him to be defensive.

"But...but why?" asked Joey.

"Because I like her...I don't know...I just do," Boyd answered.

He looked to the carpet on the ground as if he could find some further explanation in the fine thread. He found none and shrugged. Joey Horner could not contain his smile.

"What?" Boyd asked.

Joey jumped up from his sitting position and onto his feet in one motion and then darted out of the room. The other boys followed, leaving only Boyd, who had no clue what was going on. The football game had come to an end. Unfortunately for the partygoers, their team had not come out on top this time, and the taste of defeat was a bitter one that undid the taste of community and good food. Joey ran up to his father.

"Joseph, we're leaving in a bit," Joey's dad said over grumbles and groans.

"Dad, you'll never believe this," Joey said.

"What is it, Joey?" Joey's dad asked, mildly interested.

"Boyd just said he likes that black girl at our school."

The sentence silenced the room. Roger Barnaby was met with stares from every man there.

"It's all right, Roger. I hear they look more like sand people when the mamma's a darkie," someone said.

A slew of laughter swept the room. Joey's dad was coughing with laughter. He grabbed his belly and coughed out a few more.

"Could you imagine black Barnabys? 'Yo, yo, yo, what's poppin', Gramps,'" he said, causing another wave of laughter to sweep the room.

Roger Barnaby didn't take kindly to being humiliated. Just then, amid the laughter, the man of the hour emerged from his room. He looked up at all the amused faces as he fiddled around with his fingers, trying to figure out what all the fuss was about.

"Boyd Abner Barnaby, is this true?" Roger asked. His lips were pursed, and he was breathing hard through his nose.

"I don't get what the big deal is, Dad," Boyd said softly.

"What's the matter with you, Roger? You ain't teach your boy nothin'?" someone asked.

Boyd couldn't tell who though. He was looking down at the carpet again, searching for answers as strangers scolded him left and right. The scolding was stopped when his mother came into the living room, wondering what all the commotion was about.

"Now why are y'all breathin' down my boy's neck? Whatever he did wrong this time, it can't be all that bad," she said as she moved her bangs from her eyes to get a better look at the situation.

"He likes a nigger girl at school," Roger explained to his wife.

"So what's the matter with that? He'll grow out of it. I'm fine with it as long as he don't talk about her to us and keeps us in the dark," she quipped.

There were some chuckles. Men who were supposed to be heading home had grabbed themselves another beer from the cooler, which was conveniently positioned in the center of the living room right next to the television. Having been disappointed with the night's primary source of entertainment, they found new interest in the story that was playing out right in front of them.

"For the love of God, Lucy, what if the boy don't grow out of it, huh? You really want to be bringin' lady coons to the family reunions? Our son arm in arm with one of them? How do you think my parents will respond to that kind of foolery? Hell, forget my parents...think of yours."

To the guests, this simply meant that Lucy's parents were more intolerant than Roger's, but to Lucy it meant more. It was true that at some point in time Lucy's father had been a Klansman, and even after the shift in the mind-set of the civil-rights movement that had taken place just years before, he wasn't exactly reformed.

"Don't lie to yourself, Lucy. Him dating one of them when he gets older is as good as you dating one of them," Roger said.

"I hear that," someone said, and two men clanked their glasses together.

"Now, Boyd, I suppose it ain't all your fault since the government forced us in with the darkies, but you can't go 'round liking no black girls, do you understand?" Roger said to his son in a semisoothing voice. He was trying his very best to fake compassion in hopes that it would go the extra mile to convince his son.

"But why not?" Boyd asked.

"Because white people are better than black people—never forget that. That means that you would be doing yourself a disservice by keeping this little crush of yours," Roger clarified.

"But you have black friends," Boyd said.

"We all do. We can't help that. Like I said, the government forced them on us, so that's inevitable. But that's just it, Boyd. I have black friends, nothing more. They're not the kind of people I can invite over to a house party like this one. They're not the kind of people with their rap albums and criminal records that I would allow my son to associate with. They're not like us, do you understand?" Roger asked.

Something in his voice told his son that this wasn't a question to which no would be an acceptable answer.

"Yes, Dad," Boyd answered well.

Thanksgiving dissipated fairly quickly after that. The remnants of the beer cans were chugged up by the men, the last of the dirty dishes were scrubbed clean by the women, and Boyd and his friends found newer topics to talk about in the living room in the earshot of their fathers. Finally, after the men had finished their conversation on why their team had lost and why any one of them would make perfect replacements as coaches and after the last of the recipes had been exchanged, people started to leave. It played out the same way every single year. The leftovers were put in carrying bags, and the Thanksgiving smells were concealed as the women drew out their good-byes until it became long enough for whoever's husband to yell out a "Let's go!" And just like that they were gone.

"You make sure to listen to your daddy there, boy. He's a very smart man," said the Barnabys' next-door neighbor, Dale.

Dale ruffled up Boyd's hair and left. He was the last adult guest to leave. Since the Horners lived only a few houses over, Joey's parents had allowed him to stay a bit longer.

"Thanks for having me over, and thanks for the food," Joey said as he walked outside. "Oh, and Boyd, sorry if I got you in any trouble. I just thought it was funny is all."

Boyd smiled to show his forgiveness before closing the door. An adamant member of the workforce, Lucy had gone off to bed and was sound asleep. Roger sipped on the very last can of beer at the kitchen table. Boyd had had a stressful night, so he went to the kitchen to get himself some water to soothe his dry throat.

"You know you really embarrassed me today, son," Roger said.

Boyd turned around. An open newspaper hid his father's face, but Boyd could hear the loud, foamy sips.

"I'm sorry, Daddy," Boyd apologized, undoing the lid of his bottle of water.

"You just don't get it, do you?" Roger said suddenly. His voice was noticeably harsher.

Boyd took down a few gulps to water his throat, which was quickly becoming dry again.

"You don't understand what shit like that does to the reputation of a proud white man," Roger growled.

"I'm really, really sorry," Boyd apologized.

"You think having that darkie hide is 'hip'? You think it's the bee's knees, don't you?" Roger huffed.

"What's the matter?" Lucy called from their bedroom, woken by the yelling.

"Go back to sleep, you dumb bitch!" Roger yelled.

There was silence.

"You want to be black. I can make you black. I can make you black all over."

Roger put the newspaper down to reveal a pack of cigarettes.

"I'm so sorry, Pop," Boyd pleaded. He could barely see through his tears.

"Well, I ain't," Roger replied. "Boyd, roll up your sleeves."

XXIV

J osiah always told me that cops were dangerous because they were men; men are capable. Even though he was dangerous, I found that Boyd Barnaby was an amateur at being a man. He was completely lacking in better judgment. Like the innards of a tree, he had rings to mark the passage of time, only his were under his eyes instead of somewhere in his midsection. With his bevy of rings, it was hard for me to see that I was more of an adult than Boyd was. As age went up, the number of things you were insecure about tended to go down. I was many things, but hardly was I ever insecure, while Boyd reeked of insecurity. His racism was a contributing factor, but the way he policed was fueled by his insecurity. As to what he was insecure about, I had no idea. Boyd Barnaby was a bad cop because he didn't believe he was man enough to be a good one. There was danger to be found in an insecure policeman, and being around Boyd made me feel like an ant. I wasn't fooled by the police uniform that Boyd wore. I was no good guy either, but even if I was, I wouldn't have felt safe around him. He was the type to think he was the law. I'd hear it on the news about how important it was for a community to have faith in the law enforcement every time someone ended up bullet riddled and dead at the hands of the boys in blue. Although the timing of statements like that made them seem condescending, there was truth to be found in it. How Boyd policed was dangerous, but my lack of trust in him was equally dangerous in its own way. Seeds of distrust had taken root in my mind, and like all seeds they ended up growing. From sproutlet to bush, stem to trunk, seeds would always grow.

In exchange for my freedom, Boyd wanted one thing, and that was fame. He wanted to be single-handedly responsible for getting rid of a gang, and this was where I could offer him help. He needed a police report that supported his side of the story, and he prodded me until he got one out of me. But because I was underage, I needed to get it signed. Boyd would remind me. He would call my house and watch me leave school. He would remind me of how he could have me in custody at any time that he pleased. After painstakingly altering my report to Boyd's demands, and refusing to change a few details, I thought I had something. The only thing left to do was to get it signed by the one parent I had left.

I had spent another afternoon being verbally abused by Boyd at the police station and had just gotten home. After my father left, Witt had taken to living in an apartment closer to Widower's Grove. He still talked to me and took care of me more than ever before, but he couldn't stand to step foot in the house; my mother's deterioration made sure of that. I walked up my front steps and stopped to check the mailbox hanging by the door's side. I reached in and pulled out a small stack of letters. Most of them were overdue bills, which I could've guessed would be there. The sound of shattering glass broke my concentration.

"Well, here goes nothing," I said to myself.

I opened the door, and the smell of alcohol greeted me. The house was a mess; at least something was consistent. The sofa cushions were scattered throughout the living room; half of them were missing entirely. The coffee table that sat in the middle of the living room was knocked over on its side. Empty cups lay next to dry stains. The curtains that shielded the home from external judgment had been torn down, and the rips in the fabric sparked thoughts of a wild beast mauling it. The dusty ceiling fan wobbled uneasily as if traumatized by whatever events had happened. Bits and pieces of glass stuck up from the rug like shark fins in the ocean; there would be a shattered wine bottle somewhere. I walked into the kitchen with bits of glass hugging the heels of my shoes.

"Mom?" I called.

My mother had taken to drinking in secrecy; she preferred hard liquor but drank the finer kinds when she fell into her bouts of depression. She paid no attention to me and continued her muffled sobbing.

"Mamma, I know this is a bad time, but I need your help with something," I said, completely disregarding her state.

If only Pete could see us now, how little would it seem that I cared for her. I was glad he was gone for this. She was beyond help.

"Mamma, I need you to sign this," I said, placing the paperwork in front of her.

I searched the cluttered kitchen counter for a spare pen and cautiously tossed it next to the paperwork. My mother could snap in a moment without hesitation, but her depression was a safeguard I knew I had to take advantage of. There was no guarantee there would be a chance like this again.

My mother looked up at me with piercing red eyes. "He's gonna kill me one of these days, you know? Don't be surprised when he does it. One of these days, he's gonna crumple me up from the inside without so much as getting me a grave," my mother said as she grabbed the pen and looked over the paperwork.

I let out a quiet sigh. She was too disturbed to ask what it was she was signing. It wouldn't have mattered though. I doubted she would care if I filled out the statement. But she had a history with gangs in that she had grown up around them, and she knew the dangers of snitching.

"I don't know where he's run off to now. I gave the house a good tear again. I thought he was hiding," my mother said as she sloppily wrote her name in the designated spaces.

It was a sad thing to watch your own mother cry. I had had enough sadness in my life, so I avoided looking. The only sounds I could hear were scribbles as my mom jotted down her signature, the soft tapping of tears hitting paper, and the whirring sound of a ceiling fan that kept watch of it all. My mother finished signing the last few pages in silence.

"Say, what is this thing anyway?" she asked suddenly.

It was becoming apparent that the calming trance the wine had put on her was quickly starting to wear off. In the blink of an eye, my mother went from dazed and confused to aware and intense.

"What kind of nonsense are you trying to get me into?" she grumbled. She got up, holding the table for support, and lunged at me. "You think you can catch me off guard and get me to sign those divorce papers? Your father put you up to this? Huh!"

Before two steps could be taken toward me, she collapsed on the floor. Luckily, she fell unscathed by the dangerous glass pieces. She had passed out from all of the alcohol. I stepped over her unconscious body to collect the tear-stained papers, and then I turned off the lights and went to my bedroom to get a good night's rest. She slept on the floor, her arms and legs spread out like those of a shooting victim. To me, the saddest thing was that the alcohol didn't bring out someone who wasn't already there; rather, it exaggerated who was already there. She was misguided and melodramatic—which she had always been—but now she was manic as well, and that was as new as her status of being a single mother.

Sometime after turning in my friends, I was called over to Slicker's house. I wasn't worried. I had already met with Slicker several times in light of all the arrests being made. No one knew that it was me. Boyd had instructed me to notify him if any gang-related activity was taking place, in return for him keeping me from getting into legal trouble. I thought it was better to leave this meeting at Slicker's house off the record. I was already a snitch, which was a deadly thing to be where I lived. Being a police informant was the eighth sin around here.

Little did I know two people followed me that night. The first was Witt, who had seen me sneak out of the house. He was worried about me because for a few days after turning in my friends, I was silent most of the time and would only answer in nods when he asked me if I was all right. Every time he visited, things would always get worse. He saw the downward spiral in snapshots and absolutely hated it, but he decided I was worth it, so he had stopped by.

The second person to follow me that night was Boyd Barnaby. How he had known where I was going, I'll never know. Both men followed me without me knowing.

When I got to Slicker's house, I didn't even knock. The door had been left open, and I let myself in. It was dark in the house, and his place smelled like cigarettes and strong booze more so than usual. As soon as I entered his house, I was greeted with a punch.

"What the fuck do you think this is, nigga?" Slicker yelled angrily.

I dropped to the floor like a rock and covered my nose.

"You think you in school? You think this is the playground where you can just snitch on anyone you feel like?" Slicker said as he closed the door behind me. "I have an operation, lil dude, a system. Your open mouth is costing niggas time, and that is costing me money!"

My head hurt, and I could barely make sense of what he was saying.

"It's gonna cost your bitch ass a lot more though, ain't it?" he asked as he gave me a hard kick to my rib cage.

I felt something break where he had made contact. It was then I realized that there was no one else in the house—it was just me and him.

"If they ask you if you know me, you supposed to say no!" he said, giving me another kick. "If they ask again, you still say no!" Another kick. "If they ask again, you say no a third motherfucking time!" I winced. Another kick. I felt something else break.

"The worst part is I had to find out from Lamarr. Goddamn Lamarr! I was sizing him up, about to swing, and for your sake too, and you know what he told me?"

He knelt down by me and swiped his nails across my forearm where the tattoo was. Strips of my skin collected underneath his nails, and lines of blood covered the ink.

"He told me that I should really have my own gang in order before I go trying to beef with somebody else's!"

He swung his elbow down hard on my face. My left eye puffed up.

"He told me everything. Even X knew you were gonna snitch. That's why he skipped town and ghosted. Then one by one, they start taking us in. You know you're gonna die today, right?"

"Please, stop it. We're in the same group," I pleaded.

"No," said Slicker, "we was never the same."

I closed my eyes tight, pushing out tears, and waited for him to hit something important and end me. He never did.

Slicker hadn't bothered to lock his door, so when Witt barged in, the door swung open and pushed Slicker down to the ground. Witt stepped over me and gave Slicker the single greatest ass whooping I had ever heard. I turned myself over and spat out a tooth. Both of my eyes were swollen, but I could just make them out. Every punch made a sharp popping sound, like bone through a meat grinder. At one point, Slicker's cries got so loud that I thought Witt might actually kill him, but the brother had restraint and stopped himself just short. It was only after Slicker was reduced to faint whimpers that Witt turned his attention to me. I was still on the ground. I could barely move. Witt propped me up to a sitting position against the wall. He was gentle, but everything still hurt.

"What the hell have you gotten yourself into this time?" he asked. I didn't know why, but I smiled at him, and despite everything, he smiled back. It was one of the best smiles he had ever smiled, eye to eye, big and bright, so full of love.

Boyd Barnaby walked through the open door with his gun in his hands. I knew enough about him to know that he was off duty that night, and I obviously wasn't expecting him. In hearing Slicker's squeals, someone in distress, Boyd had justified having his gun ready.

The seeds grew; from sproutlet to bush, stem to trunk, the seeds grew.

I wanted to tell him that everything was fine, that my Witt had saved me, that Slicker was the ringleader, that he didn't need his gun out. I held out my hand to tell him to stop. I held out my hand quickly and in a dimly lit space.

He fired two shots. I saw Witt cry out, but I couldn't hear him because my ears were ringing. He sort of froze with his arms out to the side for a second, and then he fell to his knees. Then slowly, as though he was falling off a building, he leaned backward. He was dead when he landed. He had his eyes open. It was eight fifteen on a Friday night. I felt as though I had aged twenty years at one time. My body was heavy upon me, and my thoughts came in slow aches—adulthood in three acts and my life split in a tribalist two, and across both of those sorry pieces I didn't learn a thing.

Author's Note

Okay, if you made it this far, that means that you finished reading the book, unless you're one of those people who likes to mess around with the end of books before they start reading. In that case you're braver than me, and although I don't like what you do, I respect it. The first thing I'd like to do is thank you for reading, and I sincerely hope you enjoyed this book or at least managed to take something away from it, no matter how small.

My name is Jefta Iluyomade. I was born in Lagos, Nigeria, on April 7, 1999. I moved to the United States at around the age of four and have lived here ever since in the scenic, totally-not-boring Central Illinois area. I'm a regular teenager who writes as a hobby and a form of meditation.

As I've gone through high school, I've become more conscientious and have noticed how things are for black people, both African Americans and African people back on the continent. In short, things don't tend to go very well, but that isn't news. I noticed similarities between these two different but connected groups of people and thought I would write a story about it. While the number of things that contribute to the black struggle are too long to list, I wanted to emphasize that similar inhibitors can be experienced by Africans *and* African Americans and that unity and support within African American communities (Africans included) is invaluable. I normally don't finish my writing projects, but this one in particular meant a lot to me, so I stuck with it and finished it early 2017, after about two years of working on it on and off again.

I firmly believe that books are powerful because they lead to conversation and, in time, change. We've all seen things like police brutality and how black people are portrayed in the media. I've dealt with prejudice firsthand, I've seen it deployed against others, I've learned how systems are rigged against certain groups of people, and I've seen how a lack of respect for one's own color can become detrimental to the culture—all these things, and yet I don't have anything I would consider a concrete answer. I only have more questions. There is still so much I do not know.

Writing this has been a major learning experience, and I hope to learn still more from the writers, readers, and people who make a diverse, unified, and progressive American and African American culture so rewarding to participate in.

Thank you again for giving up a little bit of your time for my words.

—J

About the Author

Jefta Iluyomade has been influenced by a range of black artists including Bruce Onobrakpeya, Toni Morrison, Alice Walker, Chinua Achebe, and Kendrick Lamar. Born in Lagos, Nigeria, in 1999, Iluyomade moved to Illinois at age four. He spent most of his childhood in Champaign, Illinois, and attended Champaign Central High School. His extracurriculars included submissions to the school's literary magazine and being an active participant in the African American club.

Iluyomade was the winner of Phi Beta Sigma's Willie T. Summerville Book scholarship. This fall he will begin classes at the University of Illinois at Chicago.